Marcus Wilson is the author of two books, the award-winning non-fiction *Hero Street U.S.A.*, and the historical novel *Kidnapped by Columbus*, the prequel to this novel. Marc is the founder of the widely used content management system known as BLOX Digital/TownNews. Marc worked as a journalist for three daily newspapers and five bureaus of The Associated Press. He was editor/publisher/janitor of the weekly Bigfork (Montana) Eagle. He studied graduate-level history at the University of Colorado. He and his wife live in Loveland, Colorado.

To my son, Paul.

Marcus Wilson

COLUMBUS, SLAVE TRADER

AUSTIN MACAULEY PUBLISHERS™

LONDON * CAMBRIDGE * NEW YORK * SHARJAH

Ordering Information
Quantity sales: Special discounts are available on quantity purchases by corporations, associations, and others. For details, contact the publisher at the address below.

Publisher's Cataloging-in-Publication data
Wilson, Marcus
Columbus, Slave Trader

ISBN 9798886934359 (Paperback)
ISBN 9798886934366 (Hardback)
ISBN 9798886934380 (ePub e-book)
ISBN 9798886934373 (Audiobook)

Library of Congress Control Number: 2023921372

www.austinmacauley.com/us

First Published 2024
Austin Macauley Publishers LLC
40 Wall Street, 33rd Floor, Suite 3302
New York, NY 10005
USA

mail-usa@austinmacauley.com
+1 (646) 5125767

As always, my wife, Ginny, is my editor and muse. Thanks also to Bill Masterson, Gary Sosniecki, Doug Jones, and Art Stone for reading the various versions of this book, and for the steady encouragement. Credit needs to be given to the many Columbus scholars who have documented his life, helping me write a novel that is as historically accurate as possible.

Table of Contents

Note to Readers

Readers of historical fiction rightly ask: What is fiction and what is fact?

This book is a novel, but the historical events, locations and timeline are as accurate as I could make them.

An African proverb says, "Until the lion learns to write, all stories will glorify the hunter." With that in mind, I tried to tell this story from the "lion's point of view with the protagonist /narrator being a Native American."

I chose Guarocuya as the name for my narrator after the Taino cacique Enriquillo/Guarocuya, who rebelled against the Spanish on Hispaniola from 1519 to 1533.

I also drew from history, Rodrigo de Triana, who is believed to be the sailor on Columbus' 1492 voyage to first spot land in the "New World." Rodrigo's back story—that he is a banished Jew with a father imprisoned by the Inquisition—is purely fictional (although possible).

Hector, the freed slave originally from Africa, is also a purely fictional character, but his story is drawn from historical facts.

Caonabo, Anacaona and the major chiefs—caciques—named are historically accurate characters.

Queen Isabela and King Ferdinand, Columbus and his brothers—Barthlomew and Diego—are well-documented historical figures. So are Alonso de Hoja, Dr. Chanca and Fray Buil. The multiple mutineers named also are historically accurate characters.

Michele de Cuneo's letter bragging about raping a native woman is a historical document quoted accurately.

Most importantly, the failed ocean crossing with 500 natives destined for death and the slave market in Seville is a true story.

Preface

Sharks followed four tiny ships
Five hundred slaves aboard in the winter cold
Just eighty reach Seville
Sharks ate well
The first slave ships to cross the Atlantic
Carried not Blacks from east to west
But Native Americans—"Indians"—from west to east

Chapter 1
Revenge

Columbus' Grand Fleet is moored just offshore where furious Spaniards are readying spears, cannon, armor, war horses and ravenous dogs to seek revenge against my people, the Taínos.

The Spaniards are angry at the deaths the thirty-nine men Columbus left behind when he returned to Castile eleven months ago. Now the admiral has returned with a Grand Fleet—seventeen ships and 1,200 gold-crazed fortune hunters.

They expected to find gold and a Spanish settlement when they returned. Instead, they found only ashes and bearded corpses. No gold.

They are preparing to come ashore to my island to seek vengeance.

I must warn my people.

I spent nearly a year in Spain after Columbus kidnapped me and five other Taínos, and took us to Spain to prove he'd reach India. Hence, we are called 'Indians'.

I learned many things in the last year about the Spanish that bode poorly for my people. The Spanish have a rigid caste system, and they even wonder if 'Indians' are humans with souls that can be saved. Some Spaniards wonder if we are monkeys—high-level monkeys who could serve as slaves.

Their all-powerful Pope has given them authority to own our island, make us Spanish subjects and force us to give up our Gods.

From atop a bluff, I watch my friend Rodrigo pass near the ruins of *La Navidad*—Europe's first settlement in what the Spaniards call the New World. That's where Columbus found the charred bodies of the Spaniards.

I urged Rodrigo to come inland with me, but he chose to return to the fleet to try to prevent a war. But what hope does he have? He's a banished Jew who's despised by most of the men of the fleet.

Spanish honor has been challenged, and I doubt that anything Rodrigo can say will temper their thirst for revenge.

Nearly a million Taínos live on Haiti, but my people's weapons are made of stone and fish bones—no match for cannon fire, and iron-tipped spears carried by armor-clad warriors mounted on giant horses.

When the Spaniards first arrived a year ago, we Taínos thought they were gods.

Now I know most of them are demons.

Some—most?—Spaniards think Taínos are less than human. They wonder: Do we even have souls that can be saved?

Taíno gods mean nothing to the Spaniards—in fact, they think they must be destroyed. I doubt our gods can protect us from gun powder or iron spears.

My fears overwhelm me and I begin running toward Chief Guacanagari's village, about four miles to the southeast.

Everything is eerily quiet.

As I trot toward the village, no one is tending the fields of cassava or sweet potatoes. Nor is anyone weeding the gardens of squash, beans, peppers, tobacco and peanuts.

Normally, the women from the village would be weeding, watering and harvesting the crops, while children would be playing nearby. The village's men would be fishing in Caracol Bay or nearby streams.

But no one can be seen.

No one is here to cheer my return, to hear of my great adventures.

No one to warn.

Only silence.

I approach Guacanagari's village—one of the larger ones on the island. Some 500 *caneys*—small round wood and thatch huts occupied by multiple families—encircle the village square.

At the village center is Chief Guacanagari's larger rectangular home, known as a *bohio*. The chief's *bohio* houses only the chief and his family. It doubles as the village's temple during religious ceremonies.

I am stunned to see a beautiful woman standing at the door to Chief Guacanagari's *bohio*. She wears only a sheer white cotton dress that ends at her slender thighs.

After nearly a year of seeing Spanish women wearing many layers of heavy woolen clothes no matter the weather, I'm startled to see this beautiful Taíno woman.

As I near her—to my astonishment—she pulls out a dagger, and points it at me. Her face is painted for war, her face contorted with fury.

"Who are you?" she demands. "If you come closer, I kill you!"

I—still dressed as a Spanish sailor—must be as startling a site to her as she to me.

"Don't hurt me! I am Taíno! I am Guarocuya, nephew of Chief Behecchio!"

She scowls and jabs the dagger toward me again.

"Why are you dressed like that?" she demands. "Behecchio's village is far from here. No one from his village dresses like that. You dress like a rapist invader!"

"I am one of the Taínos who was kidnapped and taken to Spain. I just returned on the Spanish fleet. Their ships are anchored nearby. I'm free after nearly a year in captivity. These are the only clothes I have!"

As she watches, I rip off the clothes, leaving only a loin cloth. She watches but does not lower the dagger.

As she looks at me skeptically, I wonder, but dare not ask where she got the dagger. It wasn't made on this island.

"I've come to warn Chief Guacanagari that the Spanish have returned!"

"We need no warning!" she snarls. "We know that murdering, thieving rapists have returned!"

Hate shows in her black eyes. Fierceness makes her even more…stunning.

"I must see Guacanagari! His people must flee!"

"Are you blind? Everyone has fled—can't you tell?"

"You…you haven't."

"I am Anacaona, wife of Caonabo, the warrior who led the war against the Spaniards. The man who burned the Spanish fort, the man who killed the invaders, the rapists. I came here to promise Chief Guacanagari help if he will join us and fight the invaders!"

"Guacanagari is here?"

She scowls and looks derisively over her shoulder. She fiercely points inside the *bohio* with the dagger.

"He's inside. He claims he is wounded and cannot travel. He claims—old fool that he is—that he is a friend of Columbus. He says the admiral will not tolerate the Spaniards raping and pillaging. He claims we all will be safe now that Columbus has returned."

"I need to talk to him. To warn him that the Spanish are coming and want revenge!"

"You're wasting your time," she says but she motions with her dagger for me to enter Guacanagari's hut.

She follows me inside, her dagger aimed at my back.

The old chief lays on a wooden pallet at the far end of the hut. Standing next to him is a lean young man about my age, 15 or so.

I explain quickly that I was kidnapped, taken to Spain, but now have just returned on Columbus' fleet.

"Returned? From the land of the Spaniards?" the chief asks in astonishment, perhaps disbelief.

"Columbus and some 300 Spaniards are preparing their weapons to come here seeking revenge for the death of the men at *La Navidad!*" I warn.

"Their deaths were not my doing!" the chief declares.

He points at Anacaona.

"That was her husband! Caonabo and his warriors came into my lands and attacked and killed the Spaniards! I tried to stop them."

"You would not act to defend your own women!" Anacaona says, almost spitting with anger.

"What matters right now is that the Spaniards are marching toward this village, and they want revenge!" I say. "I'm not sure Columbus can stop them!"

"How soon?" asks the younger man, speaking for the first time.

I tell them the Spanish were bringing cannon, horses and war dogs ashore when I left the coast, just an hour or so ago. "It will take them some time to haul the cannon, up the bluff," I add.

"My people, as you can see, have already fled," the chief says. "Only my son and I remain—and this angry woman."

"I am here only to urge this old man to fight!" Anacaona says. "My husband has called for a council of chiefs—a council of war!"

"We should not kill!" Guacanagari says emphatically. "I know Admiral Columbus, he is my friend, and he is a good person. He is a man of God. He talks to God. He brings salvation and eternal life through Jesus Christ. Now that he has returned, I am sure we can all live together in peace. Our souls can be saved. We can have eternal lives!"

"You are a fool, old man!" Anacaona says. "If we don't drive the Spaniards into the sea—or into their graves—we will all end up as slaves—or dead!"

Chapter 2
Royal Robes

Leaving the chief's hut, Anacaona orders that I walk with her on a well-worn path leading into the nearby forest.

"You need to talk to my husband," she says, pointing her dagger toward the sea. "You must tell him and the council of chiefs everything you know about the evil rapists."

I nod agreement, but warn her that she should leave the village before the Spanish arrive.

"It's not going to be safe, especially for a beautiful woman!"

"We know how the evil invaders treat women!" she answers, glaring at me and waving the dagger. "You had better not be their spy!"

"I'm no spy. I can tell our people—your husband—much about the Spaniards. I was one of six Taínos taken by Columbus to Spain. I even met their queen and king."

She continues to grip the dagger with the point out, making certain I can see it.

"I could have stayed in Spain and lived in luxury at the queen's court, but instead I chose to return to help my people."

Her look remains doubtful.

"Look!" I say, pulling out the makeshift backpack I'm carrying. "These are all gifts from the queen, her children and others I met at the royal court."

I pull out the silk robe that Princess Catherine gave me. It is sheer white, nearly transparent with flares of blue and purple.

Anacaona's eyes open wide. Her look of doubt becomes one of wonder.

"What is this?" she asks in awe.

"A silk robe that was made for a princess, a future queen. She will marry the King of England and become the Queen of England, where they call her Catherine of Aragon."

Anacaona's eyes remain transfixed on the silk robe.

I offer the robe so Anacaona can touch it, but she pulls away, afraid.

"Go ahead. Hold it. It's not a trick."

Gingerly, she takes it and caresses the silk in amazement.

"Put it on!" I suggest.

She looks at me in bewilderment, so I help her into the robe, and she remains speechless.

She looks even more beautiful draped in silk. She turns around and the robe flows in the wind.

She smiles.

"You may keep it."

"Keep it?"

"I have no use for it, and it looks like it was made just for you."

The silk highlights everything about her. Everything.

We are speechless for a few moments before I add: "If you ever meet a Spaniard, show him this robe and tell him it was a gift from Princess Catalina, youngest daughter of Queen Isabela and King Ferdinand. No one would dare touch you!"

Her anger returns.

"I am the wife of Caonabo!" she says fiercely. "That is protection enough. That and my dagger! I have already used it to kill a filthy would-be rapist."

I look at her in stunned silence.

"It's the women—and men—who rely on the old fool Guacanagari who are in danger!"

She looks curiously at my backpack. "What else do you have?"

Inside is the Latin Bible and a jeweled ring Queen Isabela gave me, a robe from Prince Juan, and Rodrigo's chess set. Also, ten gold pieces, gifts from my friend the Count of Messina.

"There's no time today to show you," I say. "Someday I will show you all. You should leave now before the Spaniards arrive. No telling what will happen."

After a pause, she nods agreement.

"You'll show me everything some day?"

I promise, gladly.

"And promise you'll come to the council of the chiefs."

I nod agreement.

As she leaves, still wearing the silk robe, Guacanagari's son, standing outside his father's hut, and I watch her every movement before she disappears into the forest.

The chief has risen from the floor, and stands at the door.

"She may not look it, but she's old enough to be your mother," the chief says with a smile. "She has a daughter just a bit younger than both of you."

After a moment's thought about the daughter, I ask: "Where did she get that dagger—the beautiful little knife she had?"

"You don't want to know," he answers. "Just know it has Spanish blood on it."

Chapter 3
Chief's son

Chief Guacanagari orders his son and me to see how the Spaniards are progressing.

As we stride toward the sea, I tell the chief's son, "My name is Guarocuya. But the Spanish call me Enriquillo."

"I am Tuaymi, only son of Guacanagari. Why do you have a Spanish name?"

I tell him I was one of six Taínos tricked by the Spaniards into boarding their ship, *La Nina.* "They lifted anchor and sailed away without letting us return to our homes."

"Why would they do that?"

"Columbus believed he had reached a land called India. He wanted to bring 'Indians' back to Spain to prove he'd reached India," I answer. "We traveled hundreds of miles through Spain so Columbus could show off his 'Indians'."

"Tell me more," Tuaymi says.

"We survived great ocean storms before we reached a land called Portugal, where we met the King of Portugal. We then sailed to the small Spanish port of Palos, where two of the six Taínos died of disease. Three other Taínos and I traveled many miles across Spain to the royal court in a large city called Barcelona, where we met the queen and king of Spain, and many other high-ranking people. We four Taínos were baptized—without anyone asking us—into the Christian church. At that time, the Spanish gave me the name Enriquillo in honor of the queen's dead older brother."

"Incredible!" Tuaymi says, looking at me in awe.

It is my turn to ask questions. "Why are you and your father still here?"

Tuaymi takes a deep breath and looks out at the horizon before answering.

"My father met Admiral Columbus last year, and he trusts him. The admiral told him about Christianity, and my father now believes in the One God and his son Jesus. And he believes in Columbus, who says he talks to God. My father asks how anyone can doubt a man who talks with their God? He believes his soul—our souls—can be saved, and we can have eternal life."

"What do you think of that?"

"I still believe in our gods," Tuaymi says. "Do you still believe in our gods?"

"Yes. But tell me more about your father."

"He is my father, and I am not going to leave him here to meet the Spaniards alone. I hope my father and Admiral Columbus can achieve peace. I'm fearful that Caonabo and Anacaona are right. Everyone cheers for Caonabo now, and many Taínos disdain my father."

We reach a bluff overlooking the sea.

We can see about 200 Spaniards in formal military formation slowly advancing through the marsh toward Guacanagari's village. Horses pulling cannons flounder in the marsh. Men in full armor swat mosquitos. As they approach, we hear the music of pipes and drums.

"They could easily have avoided the marsh," Tuaymi says with muted amusement.

I grunt agreement, as I just traveled the same route, but skirted the swamp, the mud, and mosquitos. There is a clear path.

"Do you know any of them?" Tuaymi asks.

"Columbus is in the front, dressed in his formal Admiral of the Ocean Sea uniform. Not in armor. That's a good sign."

"Why a good sign?"

"It means he's coming to formally pay homage to your father, whom he calls the King of Hispaniola."

"If he's just coming to pay homage, why is he bringing all the weapons?"

"Columbus has to show his own men that he is serious about the loss of the Spaniards at *La Navidad*. If your father can provide good answers, perhaps there will be no problems."

"What if my father's answers aren't good enough?"

He shrugs. "Let's hope we don't find out."

"Who else do you recognize?" he asks.

"There's Dr. Chama, a medical man, and a good man. I see Fray Buil, a Benedictine monk who is the highest-ranking religious man in the fleet, and the person charged by the king and queen with baptizing the natives of this island. But from what I hear, he has no love for people he considers his inferiors. And he considers almost everyone his inferior."

"We are considered inferior?" Tuaymi asks.

I hesitate before I tell him: "There were some at court who wondered aloud if we Taínos are monkeys."

"Monkeys? What are monkeys?"

"I'm not sure, but I understand they are an animal that is less than a human. They are animals without souls that can be saved."

As the Spaniards draw nearer, I point out Alonso de Hojeda. "He is a very ambitious man, a very treacherous man who should not be trusted. His uncle was one of the founders of the Spanish Inquisition."

"Inquisition?"

"Part of the Catholic Church that was established to maintain purity of thought. Very powerful and dangerous in Spain." I don't tell him about the Inquisition burning humans at the stake.

We watch in silence for several minutes before Tuaymi asks: "Can any of the men coming toward us be trusted?"

I look hard, and near the back of the Spanish military formation I spot Rodrigo.

I smile.

"There is at least one among them who can be trusted. He is a Jew who helped me and the other kidnapped Taínos survive the trip to Spain."

"What's a Jew?" Tuaymi asks.

"They are a people who have been banished from Spain because they don't believe in the Christian savior Jesus Christ. But they do believe in the Christian God."

"What's the Jew's name?"

"Rodrigo de Triana. He's my friend."

Chapter 4
Columbus Visits

As the Spanish slowly draw near, we retreat back to the village.

Tuaymi slows down, turns to me and says, "You'd better hide your packet of goods. The Spaniards steal anything they find."

Gifts from Queen Isabela, Prince Juan and the Count and Countess of Messina should be safe from those who came on behalf of the royal Spanish court.

Columbus should help me protect the gifts. He knows I am the queen's godson.

But can I be sure?

Greedy Spaniards would certainly desire the ten gold doubloons the count gave me—and the royal ring, and very rare Bible.

"You're right. Where can I hide all this?"

He points with his right arm and says, "Follow me!"

We trot away from the sea toward higher ground, following the trace of a trail that leads to the entrance to a deep cavern hidden in the middle of a tangled grove of banyan trees.

"This, as you know, is scared ground, home to our gods. Maybe they will help protect your things."

Our gods Boinael and Maroya emerged from caverns—maybe even this one—to bring light to the Earth, Boinael controlling the sun, and Maroya controlling the moon. That's how we were created.

Saying prayers silently to the ancient gods, I climb into their sacred domain to hide my treasures. Will the gods be angry with me, or pleased that I am defying the Spaniards' God?

Sliding into the cavern until there is little daylight left, I hide my pack—including my old Spanish clothes—in a hole behind a damp rock. Will I ever see these treasures again? I'm glad I gave Anacaona the princess' robe.

As we return to the village, Tuaymi tells me: "If anyone asks, we'll tell the Spaniards you are my father's nephew, and my cousin." I nod agreement.

Looking at the chief's son, I have a good feeling I've made a new friend.

Columbus and the Spaniards are less than one-half mile away when we return to the village. We tell Guacanagari what we saw and learned. He agrees with a shrug to the story that I'm his nephew.

The three of us watch as the Spaniards' military column advances.

"I think Columbus comes in peace, but others want revenge," I say. "They have weapons you've never seen, and some of the Spaniards will want to use them as a matter of honor."

"Columbus is a peaceful man," Guacanagari says. "He is a man of God—he speaks to God. He carries the word of Jesus, the savior."

"There may be a mutiny brewing against Columbus," I mutter. I fear that whatever Columbus says or wants may not matter.

"What's a mutiny?" Tuaymi asks.

"It's when the followers rebel against their leader."

"Why would they do that?" the chief asks.

"Columbus made many promises. He promised that gold would be easy to find, and that the Spaniards at *La Navidad* would welcome the returning fleet with gold, cannon salutes and food. Now they arrive after crossing the ocean with little food left, and they find the Spanish fortress burned and their men dead. And—perhaps most importantly—there's no gold."

As the Spaniards draw near, we see many of the men in the formation drop out and go into the abandoned huts.

"Just like the men at *Navidad*, these Spaniards are looking to steal gold, food and women," Tuaymi says in a contemptuous near-whisper.

Columbus and several of his men march straight to Guacanagari's hut. I can see that the chief is shaking with fear. As the Spaniards draw near, he slips back into his hut and lies on his mat and covers himself with a cotton cloth.

Tuaymi whispers to me, "Our story is that my father was wounded trying to protect the Spaniards at *La Navidad*, and that's why he hasn't come to the beach to greet Columbus."

"Was he wounded?"

Tuaymi doesn't answer.

So it is left to Tuaymi and me to greet Columbus and his men. I wonder if any of them will recognize me. Probably not, as I crossed the ocean on the *Nina*, and had little contact with the crews on the other 16 ships.

Dr. Chanca, Hojeda, Fray Bull and Rodrigo—accompany Columbus as he reaches Chief Guacanagari's hut. The other Spaniards are ransacking the abandoned huts.

Columbus bows politely, and says, "We are here to see his lordship, King Guacanagari."

"I am his son, and this is his nephew," Tuaymi says, remarkably calmly. We return bows.

I nod slightly to Rodrigo, and a look of surprise quickly disappears from his face. He and I allow the others to go inside the chief's hut before we follow slowly behind.

"I'm glad you're here," I whisper to Rodrigo in Taíno.

He smiles slightly and whispers in Taíno, "Prepare for trouble."

Inside, Guacanagari makes a half-hearted effort to rise, groans and falls back onto his bed.

"I am happy to come to see you, my friend," Columbus says, bowing again. Rodrigo translates. "Fortunately, since the last time we met, this young man here, Rodrigo de Triana, has learned your language, so we can talk more easily than before."

The chief nods toward Rodrigo, and they exchange smiles. The cloth mostly covers his trembling.

"Welcome, my friend, Lord Admiral," the chief says. "Forgive me for not rising, and for not meeting you at your fleet, but I was injured trying to help the Spaniards at the fortress. My leg is wrapped to help my wound heal."

"What happened at the fort? And to the men I left under your protection?" Columbus asks Guacanagari in a stern voice.

Guacanagari tells Columbus that the Spaniards at *Navidad* marauded across the island stealing gold, food and women. Each Spaniard wanted five women. If Taínos fought back, the Spaniards killed or maimed them. Or both.

"If they didn't kill them, they cut off their hands and ears and noses, and left them to bleed to death!" Tuaymi adds. He points to his right ear lobe, which was missing. "They did this to the son of their best friend among the Taínos."

I'm stunned. I hadn't noticed my new friend's mutilated ear.

"Admiral Columbus, I talked many times to your friend, Diego he Harana, whom you left in charge," Guacanagari says. "He was a good man, the cousin of your woman. He tried to control his men, but they wouldn't listen to him. Some of the Spanish men killed him! After he died no one was in charge."

Columbus looks shocked. "Spaniards killed Diego?"

The chief nods.

"My father tried hard to keep the peace," Tuaymi adds, "but when the Spaniards went into the territory controlled by Chief Caonabo hunting for gold and women there was nothing he could do."

"The Spaniards saw Caonabo's beautiful wife and daughter, and when they tried to take them Caonabo and his men grabbed them and killed them," Tuaymi adds.

Columbus asks what happened to the rest of the Spaniards.

"Caonabo brought many men together, and they had a war council, and they decided to burn the fortress and kill the rest of the Spaniards," Tuaymi says. "There was little my father could do against the anger of all the Taínos."

"Did you try to stop them?" Columbus asks Guacanagari, who mumbles an answer.

"My father tried, and he lost the respect of many of the Taínos on the island for siding with the Spaniards," Tuaymi says. "Caonabo is now the most important chief on the island."

Guacanagari glares at his son, angry that he praised Caonabo.

"I tried to stop them! I was injured trying to stop Caonabo's men!" Guacanagari says loudly, half rising from his bed.

Fray Buil speaks for the first time: "He's lying!"

"I agree!" says Hojeda, brandishing a sword. "He's a liar and a murderer, and a heathen. Let's burn him at the stake as a warning to all the other pagans!"

"We should take our cannons and blow up the whole village, and burn these three at the stake to show the rest of the Indians we are not to be stopped from doing God's work," thunders Buil.

Rodrigo doesn't translate their threats into Taíno. But the chief and his son sense the anger.

"Remember you are here, Fray Buil, to save—not kill—souls. A burning would likely mean an end to all friendship with the Taínos," Dr. Chanca says quietly to the burley monk, who only scowls back.

Columbus points to Guacanagari and says: "This man, my friend, was wounded defending the queen's fortress. He is a king. We should treat him as a hero."

"If we are going to survive here on this island, we are going to need the help of the natives," adds Dr. Chanca.

"Let's have Dr. Chanca examine King Guacanagari's wound," Rodrigo suggests.

I'm shocked. I whisper to him in Taíno: "I'm not certain he is injured."

Rodrigo blinks in surprise, and pauses before saying in Taíno, "I think we can trust the doctor."

"We need to clear the hut so Dr. Chanca will have enough room and light for his examination," Rodrigo says. "I will stay to translate."

He points to me, "Please stand just inside the door and hold it open so the doctor has plenty of light."

Columbus nods agreement. Grumbling in protest, Buil and Hojeda follow the admiral out. I nod for Tuaymi to leave too, and he does so, also grudgingly.

Alone, Rodrigo whispers to Dr. Chanca: "Doctor, did you take the Hippocratic Oath?"

The doctor looks curiously at Rodrigo.

Rodrigo sighs with relief, and asks Dr. Chanca, "Does that oath not say 'in whatever house I enter, I will enter to help the sick, and I will abstain from all intentional wrong-doing and harm'?"

"Yes, it does," the doctor answers, surprised. "How do you know?"

"I, too, studied medicine before my people were expelled from Spain. So, I know that the Hippocratic Oath also says 'whatsoever I shall see or hear in the course of my profession, I will never divulge, holding such things to be holy secrets'."

"That's correct," Chanca answers with a nod, adding: "I know that many of Spain's best doctors were Jews."

"We need your help, doctor. You would be doing great harm, massive harm, possibly destroying innocent people and causing war between the Spanish and the Taínos if you find that Chief Guacanagari isn't injured. As his doctor, you mustn't divulge his secrets."

After a brief pause and a slight frown, Chanca nods agreement before unwrapping the cotton bandage. He sees no wound.

"Looks like he's a rapid healer, wouldn't you say, doctor?" Rodrigo says in a low voice.

Chanca nods, rewraps the bandage and slowly walks outside the hut where Columbus and the others wait.

"He's healing extraordinarily well! Remarkably well, I would say!" says the doctor.

Columbus nods, bows to Guacanagari, and says, "Thank you, my friend, for your efforts to protect my men! I am pleased that you are healing well and can be trusted."

The admiral glances at Chanca and Rodrigo. Buil and Hojeda are gone, perhaps looking for loot, perhaps secretly plotting mutiny.

"Back to the ships, Admiral?" Rodrigo suggests.

Columbus smiles in relief, and orders his men to reform. From somewhere, a horn sounds, and the Spaniards gather after a time in formal military formation, and return, drums and fifes sounding.

What few items that had been left in the village's huts are gone.

But, for the moment at least, there is peace.

Just before the Spaniards depart, I tell Rodrigo of the plans for a council of chiefs.

"I'll try to attend," Rodrigo whispers to me. "No one on the fleet will miss me."

Chapter 5
Homecoming

The next morning, as I begin my trip to my home village, my brain overloads with thoughts of Spain, Queen Isabela, Columbus, Anacaona's dagger, Rodrigo, the chiefs' war council, the bodies of the burned Spaniards, cannons and war horses—and my people's weapons made of wood and stone.

The Spanish think we are monkeys—less-than-human creatures without souls—creatures best suited to be slaves.

In an effort to cheer myself, I imagine my parents' and friends' surprise when I return—from another world, even from the dead.

What stories I'll have to tell!

I saw marvels I could never have imagined—great cities, cathedrals, castles and vast estates. I met kings and princes, dukes and marquises, ambassadors and bishops. I made great friends—Rodrigo, and the count and countess of Messina. I became godson of the king and queen of Spain. I learned to ride—and love—a horse! Queen Isabela, my godmother, said I could study under some of the great masters of Europe, be friends with her children who were destined to be kings and queens, and never want for anything.

Except I would always want to be among my own people, want to have a wife and children.

So, I chose to return where I belong. My fear is that 'where I belong' will soon be destroyed.

Returning home, I feel like I've traveled back in time. Two completely different worlds sharing the same planet. Can they co-exist?

Now I'm back, and my thoughts turn to my family and friends.

My father, Maniocatex, taught me how to fish the rivers and canoe in the sea, and how to use stealth and a bow and arrow to hunt birds. He taught me how to play sports, and how to win and lose with grace. He taught me right from wrong.

We are not monkeys.

My father is the chief of our small village, and his older brother, Bohechio, is the most important chief in the western-most part of our island. My mission is to alert Bohechio and my father about the return of Columbus and the Spanish, and to get them to attend the council of chiefs.

I have thought much about my father since Rodrigo shared with me the doom that his father faced—disappearing into the Inquisition's dungeons. Or worse.

My father doesn't know that I live. That will soon change—a thought that lifts gloom from my heart.

After three days and two nights of travel, I reach our village two hours after sunset. A near full moon is rising.

I want to find my father without others noticing my arrival, which is certain to cause a great stir.

I know that my father takes a solitary walk each evening along the creek that borders our village, and I wait for him behind a tangle of banyans next to the creek.

"Father," I call out quietly as he approaches. He is startled, and looks in all directions but doesn't see me amid the moon shadows.

"Father, it is me, Guarocuya!"

As I step out from behind the trees, he steps back in terror. Then a great smile crosses his weathered face, and he reaches out and pulls me to his body and hugs me and hugs me until I am breathless. I hug back equally hard.

"I knew you would return," he says. "Everyone was sure you were dead, lost to Bagua, god of the sea. But your mother told me every night that you still lived. She could feel your heart beat—always since you left!"

"How is she?"

"Better now that you've returned!"

We sit on a log, and, with the stream's roar as a background. The moonlight lets me study his sharp, narrow face. I recount quickly my trip to Spain and back, and the need to have the chiefs of the island meet to decide how to deal with Columbus and the Spanish.

I ask him to go with me to see his brother.

"Let's return to our village first, so your mother will know you have returned safely."

"Let's go to your brother's village first, tell him what's happened, urge him to go to the chiefs' council, then we can return and see mother. If I return home now, there will be too much commotion."

"Your mother will be angry with me," my father says, "but you are right."

Without another word, we rise and trot to my uncle's village some three miles away, which we enter without attracting notice.

"Maniocatex, my brother, what a surprise," Chief Behecchio says.

Then his eyes widen in terror as they focus on me.

"Guacocuya! Is that really you?" he asks in astonishment. He rubs his eyes.

I tell him quickly all that has happened since I returned.

Behecchio is silent for a few moments before saying, "We all have heard about *La Navidad*. Some of my men joined Caonabo—and all now celebrate his victory—and sneer at Guacanagari as a weak old woman afraid of shadows."

"Guacanagari says he will attend the council of chiefs and argue that we can have peace with Columbus," I say.

"How do you know this?" Behecchio asks.

"I talked with Guacanagari, and with Caonabo's wife, Anacaona, who says she and her husband want to fight the Spaniards."

"I hear Anacaona killed the Spaniard who tried to rape her daughter— killed him with his own dagger," my father says.

That explains the dagger. Taken from a dead man. A Spaniard. A would-be rapist.

Behecchio asks, "Where are the Spaniards now?"

"The Spanish have abandoned *Navidad* and their fleet is sailing east looking for the site of a new settlement."

"When is the council of chiefs?" he asks.

"As soon as possible. At Caonabo's village."

"I will be ready to leave the day after tomorrow," my uncle says. "Maniocatex, I hope you will accompany me. The chiefs will all want Guacocuya to tell us everything he can about Columbus and the return of the Spaniards."

My father and I return to our home village.

My mother, Ceruia, and I were always especially close. She's always hugged me in her own special way. She collapses her entire body around me, like she's capturing me.

When my father and I return to our village, it is nearly midnight. Everyone is asleep, except for my mother, unable to sleep because of her husband's absence.

She's waiting outside the door of our hut, and when she sees me, she rushes forward and surrounds me with her special hug.

Tears stream down her face.

"You told me he'd come back!" my father keeps saying.

"I knew he was alive," she whispers between sobs. "I feel his heart beat."

To avoid waking neighbors, we enter our family hut. My little sister sleeps in the far corner.

"We prayed for you every night," mother says.

"And I prayed for you every night."

"We watched when you swam out to the Spanish ship," father says. "We waited for you to swim back to shore, but then the Spanish ship sailed away. I took a canoe and tried to follow the ship, but it sailed much faster than I could paddle."

Mother, after choking down another sob, adds, "We stayed on the beach for many days hoping the ship—and you—would return."

"I've always known when your heart was beating," mother adds. "I never told you this, but when you were born, you were born many weeks too early. You had a twin sister."

I remember my dead twin. Somehow, we talked to each other in the womb. Before she died, she made me promise to carry her spirit—but her spirit refused to go with me to Spain. She warned me not to go on the Spanish ship, but I wouldn't listen.

"Your twin sister was stillborn. I held her and knew she was dead. Then you came, and the old women said you, too, were stillborn. But I held you, and could tell you were alive. Only I could feel your heart beat."

Father adds, "The old women said your mother had gone crazy with grief. They said you were born blue and cold, and that your heart wasn't beating. They wanted to take you away and bury you in the forest, along with your twin."

"What?" I ask in astonishment.

"It's true," father says.

"But I took you in my arms—you were so tiny—and I put my ear to your chest, and I could hear your heart beating when no one else could. It was very faint, but I could hear it. I listened for your breath, and I could feel it, though it was very faint."

"Each day the old women came for your body," father said.

"I begged your father to drive them away. And he did," mother said amid sobs of joy.

"Your mother laid down with you and surrounded your body," father says. "It was like you were still in her womb."

"I took big breaths, and put my mouth to your mouth and blew air into your lungs. I did that over and over, and you started breathing! Your heart beat a little stronger every day. Finally, your father could feel it."

I'm too stunned to say anything.

"You started to nurse a little bit, and your heart beat stronger. You breathed a little better every day. But the old women didn't believe me, and they came every day for your corpse."

My father nods.

"Then one day," he says, "you started crying. Everyone in the village— even the old women—came outside our hut to hear you cry. They all thought it was a miracle, and they all said many prayers to our gods. They said you'd come back from the dead."

And now I have returned from the dead. Again.

Chapter 6
Caonabo

We leave early in the morning from Behecchio's village, which is south of a range of mountains that runs at an angle from the middle of Haiti—the Spanish call our island Hispaniola—to the sea northwest of the village.

I find joy traveling with my father and uncle through this beautiful land of mountains, forests and rivers. While surrounded by these beautiful sights, I spend much of the time telling them about our trip across Spain that Columbus took from Palos to Barcelona. My uncle and father marvel at the wonders I saw, and the great figures I met.

I ask them about Caonabo's war against the Spaniards, but they say only: "You can ask Caonabo himself in a couple of days."

My father does tell me that Caonabo is 'the most cheerful of men—until you make him mad! Then watch out!'

I want to know more about the story of Anacaona knifing a Spaniard to death, but my uncle says, "All I've heard is gossip."

To reach Caonabo's village we hike along the northern edge of a large lake with mountains towering above our left. The trail leads us to a passage in the mountains that will allow us to reach Caonabo's village without scaling mountains that reach as high as 10,000 feet.

Caonabo's village, one of the largest on the island, lies in a magnificent valley between two mountain ranges. Everywhere we go we meet friendly Taínos—quite the contrast from when I, traveling with Columbus, marched across the barren, tree-less plains of Castile filled with sullen, war-weary people.

I can't help but contrast Haiti with Castile and Aragon. Taínos live together in grass and thatch huts, often with multiple families sharing the same hut. In

Spain, the rich live in huge castles and mansions, while the poor often live in squalor.

Food is grown and shared freely among Taínos. We have few class distinctions, while the Spanish calculated almost every conversation around their caste system. Spaniards hunger for gold, while Taínos see little value in gold. Taínos see gods everywhere, and we worship zemis great and small. Spaniards have only one great all-powerful God—and they want all other gods vanquished. Each village and each person can have a zemi, while in Spain any who worship any god but the One God and His Son can be punished, even with death.

***

The sun is setting when we arrive at Caonabo's village on our second day of travel. Guacanagari and Guarionex have already arrived, but the two other principal chiefs—Mayobanex and Higuayo—have not.

We are all pleased that Guacanagari—who has feuded with Caonabo—has decided to come, and I'm glad to see his son, Tuaymi, again.

To my disappointment, my friend Rodrigo hasn't arrived.

Caonabo greets my father and uncle with hugs, but doesn't touch or acknowledge me. I detect a scowl.

After talking to my uncle and father, Caonabo points to me and says, "I'd like to talk to you. Alone."

My father and uncle look at me in puzzlement as I walk away with Caonabo.

After we enter his *bohio*, Caonabo reaches down,—and to my surprise—picks up and unfolds the silk robe I'd given Anacaona.

"Explain," he says in a stern voice.

I'm startled.

I'm not sure where to begin. Am I being confronted by a jealous husband? By a man I've been warned not to anger?

"It's complicated."

"You gave this to my wife. I want to know where it came from, but more especially why you gave it to her!"

I quickly and nervously recount my trip to Spain, and the gifts given to me by the queen and her children.

"I don't understand," Caonabo says impatiently.

"The queen learned that I am the nephew of Behecchio, who Columbus says is one of the kings of this island. The queen decided that I am a royal prince. So she and her children, and others at court, gave me gifts so I could dress like royalty."

"This is one of gifts?" Caonabo asks.

"Yes. The queen's son—Prince Juan—and four daughters wear different robes every day. As gifts to me so I would be dressed as a prince, the queen's children gave me robes."

"So," Caonabo asks, "you brought these robes here when you returned?"

"Two of them, yes."

Caonabo is silent for several minutes. "I think I understand where this robe came from, but what I still don't understand is why you gave it to my wife. This is a very beautiful and precious thing."

I nod but say no more.

"Why did you give it to her?" he demands, staring with me with fiery dark eyes.

I can't tell her husband that when I saw his wife, I thought she was the most beautiful woman I'd ever seen, and that I wanted to impress her with a magnificent gift. I need a safer answer.

Caonabo gestures with his hands and scowl for me to explain.

"I have no use for the robe now that I have returned. But I don't want it to go to waste."

Caonabo purses his lips, not fully accepting my story.

"When I learned she's your wife, I thought it would honor you if I gave her the robe."

"Are you finished?" he asks, a wry smile on his face.

I continue: "I thought if she was ever in trouble with the Spanish invaders, she could show them the robe as proof that she has ties to Queen Isabela's court. That might give her some protection."

"You should know," Caonabo says in a low tone, "that she is quite capable of taking care of herself."

I remember learning that she killed a Spaniard with his own dagger—but I say nothing except, "It was my pleasure to give your wife the robes."

Caonabo shows a slight smile, rises and points me toward the door.

As I leave Caonabo's hut, my father is waiting for me.

"You have a fine, generous son," Caonabo tells my father. "He's been on a great adventure, and let's hope his knowledge can help us deal with the Spaniards."

"What was that about?" my father asks after we walk away from Caonabo's hut.

"I'll explain later." I hope he forgets to ask me.

***

Everyone is curious about my trip to Spain, so while we wait for the rest of the chiefs to arrive, I recount my story.

Almost everyone in the village gathers in the open space in front of Caonabo's bohio to hear my tale. The chiefs sit closest, then the village priests, and the elders. Children sneak ever closer to hear better. I note that Anacaona is sitting next to her husband, a small smile on her face.

I've always been a bit shy and quiet, and it's odd now to be the center of everyone's curiosity.

Before I begin, my father warns me to be careful about what I say. "You don't want to frighten the people."

I begin by telling them there were six Taínos aboard *La Nina*, when it hoisted anchor and sailed for Spain.

We were joined at sea by another Spanish ship, the *Pinta*, and the two ships sailed together until a terrible storm struck in the middle of the ocean. When the storm finally ended, we could no longer see the *Pinta*, and we believed she'd sunk.

Our badly damaged ship somehow arrived in a land called Portugal. Our ship was repaired in a great port city called Lisbon. While the ship was being repaired, Columbus and some of his party—including me, the only Taíno who wasn't near death from seasickness—traveled to see the king of Portugal. He was very curious and outwardly friendly, but Columbus learned that some of the king's men—and maybe the king himself—wanted to kill us.

After the ship was repaired, we sailed to the small Spanish port of Palos. We were treated very well at a place called *La Rabida* monastery, which is a home of kindly religious men called Franciscans.

I tell my audience that the monks gave me an animal—a small horse named Sisi that I learn to ride and love. The children seem especially amused by my stories about Sisi.

I tell the story of arriving in the great Spanish city of Seville during the Christians' most important holiday, Holy Week and Easter. I tell of climbing to the top of a great cathedral in Seville, but—remembering my father's warning—I don't tell them that from the top of the cathedral I saw the place where some two thousand people had been burned alive by the Spanish Inquisition.

Did you meet kind people? I'm asked.

Indeed. My favorite person, Rodrigo de Triana, learned to speak Taíno from me, and taught me how to speak Spanish. The crowd marvels that I can speak the Spaniard's language.

I tell my audience that Rodrigo may be one of the most educated, kindest persons in the world, and that he likely will soon visit this village. A murmur sweeps through my audience.

"You should treat Rodrigo with great respect and kindness," I add.

I tell my people about the many kindnesses shown me by the Count and Countess of Messina, some of the richest people in the world.

I tell about traveling with Columbus to the mighty city of Cordoba, which has a magnificent church that was once one of the major Muslim shrines in the world.

In Cordoba, I say, I met Admiral Columbus' beautiful woman, Beatriz de Harana. Remembering my father's warning, I don't say that her cousin was one of the men killed at *Navidad.*

After we eat our midday meal, I resume my story to an audience even larger than before. Taínos from neighboring villages have traveled to hear my story. I note that beautiful Anacaona has moved closer to me. I must be careful.

I tell my audience that we traveled by foot and on horseback more than 600 miles across Spain. We stayed at many famous and forbidding castles, and at regal monasteries. Dukes, earls, counts and bishops hosted us. We had great feasts and parades.

I next tell the story of our arrival at the royal court of Queen Isabela of Castile and King Ferdinand of Aragon in Barcelona. I tell how the Taínos were treated with great kindness, especially by the Queen, who gave us many gifts. I avoid telling about the forced baptisms of the Tainos.

"Enough story-telling," my father tells me at the end of the day. "We have to get prepared for the council of chiefs. You will have to retell everything to the chiefs after they all arrive."

At my father's suggestion, I'd left out the scariest parts of my story—the burnings, the diseases that claimed two Taínos' lives, the Spanish caste system, the Inquisition, our forced baptisms, and that many Spaniards at court doubt that Taínos are human.

Who here would even know what a monkey is? Or that some Spaniards think we'd be good slaves.

But I will tell the chiefs all. They need to know everything. They need to know the worst: The Pope's ruling that the Spanish own our land, the questions about Taínos being monkeys without souls, the expulsion of the Jews, and the defeat, the hatred of other gods, and humbling of the Moors.

And the Inquisition, burnings at the stake, monkeys and slaves.

Chapter 7
The Chiefs' Council

I'm delighted when Rodrigo arrives in the village the next day, but Caonabo treats him with suspicion and hostility.

Forgetting that I told him Rodrigo speaks Taíno, he rants: "The last time Spaniards came into my village they tried to steal and rape my wife, daughter and other women. They maimed my men!"

He stares at Rodrigo, and a cloud of anger crosses his face. "We had to kill them. Now, another has arrived!"

Rodrigo looks to me for help.

I tell Caonabo that Rodrigo isn't like the other Spaniards, and remind him that Rodrigo protected the six Taínos that Columbus kidnapped, that he learned to speak Taíno, that his people—the Jews—had been banished from Spain, that his father was imprisoned and may have been killed by the Spanish.

"You speak our language?" Caonabo demands, doubt in his voice.

"I do," Rodrigo answers.

"And the Spanish killed your father?" Caonabo asks, his voice softening.

"I don't know for certain. Maybe they killed him," Rodrigo answers in Taino. "They imprisoned him for certain."

"He was locked away in the dungeons—the torture chambers—of the Inquisition in Seville!" I add for emphasis. "Rodrigo is tortured because he can't find out what really happened to his father."

Rodrigo motions with both hands for me to say no more.

Caonabo's scowl fades, and he says, "Tell me about your father."

"He was the leader—the rabbi—of Jewish people in Seville. When the Jews were banished from that city, my father went to the Spanish authorities armed with stacks of legal documents and tried to talk to them, to reason with them, to discuss the law. I was a young boy of nine, and I watched him go into their castle. He never came out."

"Rodrigo even tried to sneak into the castle to find his father—but I stopped him!" I add, causing Rodrigo again to motion me to silence. But Caonabo needs to know.

"What are Jewish people?" Caonabo asks Rodrigo.

"We were a minority of people in Spain who believe in the same God as the Christians, but not in their savior, Jesus Christ. Throughout history, Jews have been persecuted."

"Your father was captured when he just tried to talk? Because he wanted to reason with the Spanish?" Caonabo asks.

I interrupt and tell the chief that the 'Spanish Inquisition has put thousands of people to death by burning them alive—for being different'.

"Burned alive?" Caonabo asks in a low tone.

He is silent for several minutes before looking at Rodrigo and saying, "Your father was a brave man. His story proves to me that it isn't possible to negotiate with the Spanish, although my friend, Chief Guacanagari, thinks we can."

"My father was indeed a brave man," Rodrigo agrees in a near whisper.

"Quite a story," Caonabo responds. "You, too, are a brave man to walk into my village alone, knowing that we killed the Spaniards at *Navidad*."

"Rodrigo is the best man I know," I say, looking into Caonabo's eyes.

"That is a great compliment, considering what good men your father and uncle are," Caonabo tells me.

"They are indeed good and brave men, but they haven't endured what Rodrigo has endured."

He looks Rodrigo in his eyes and says, "If you are as good a man as Guarocuya says I would be a fool not listen to you."

"If you will let me, I will do my best to be your friend, and friend to your people," Rodrigo answers.

"Your words are fair, but only your actions will matter," Caonabo answers.

Two days later, after all the chiefs have arrived, the council begins in Caonabo's *bohio*. Caonabo sits in the middle, flanked by Higuayo, Behecchio, Guarionex, Mayobanex and Guacanagari.

My father, as a lesser chief, sits on the edge with Anacaona and other lesser chiefs. As a sign of great respect, both Rodrigo and I are allowed to attend, and sit behind Anacaona and my father.

Caonabo begins by welcoming Rodrigo, and asking him to tell the story of his father trying to reason with the Spanish authorities.

After Rodrigo does so, Caonabo nods approvingly to Rodrigo, and says, "From this story we know how the Spaniards treat people who are different than they are. I don't think we were wrong to kill the Spaniards."

"Let us not be hasty in our judgments," cautions Guacanagari. "I believe we can trust Admiral Columbus and his savior, Jesus Christ. They offer eternal life!"

Caonabo nods courteously to Guacanagari before asking me to tell the council about my kidnapping, and forced conversion to the Spaniards' religion. I repeat much of what I'd said, and close with the story that some of the Spaniards wanted to burn me alive on the beach after they found *Navidad* in ashes.

"They wanted to tie me to a stake and burn me alive as a warning to all the Taínos," I say.

"They would do that to someone who is the godson of the king and queen?" Caonabo asks.

"Columbus stopped them from killing me because I am the queen's godson."

"You see," says Chief Guacanagari, "Columbus is a good man, and he can control the Spaniards. I still believe we must try to be friends. He speaks directly to the Christian's One God. We can have peace with Columbus and his men. "

Many voices start speaking at once until Caonabo raises his right hand for silence.

"That's why we meet here today," he says. "I think we need to prepare for war, while my friend Guacanagari says we should try to befriend the invaders. I hope we can all reach agreement."

Caonabo asks Rodrigo to tell the council what he knows about Columbus' intentions.

"The Spanish have abandoned *Navidad* and are looking for a better site for a new settlement and fortress," Rodrigo says.

He tells them the Spanish fleet has been trying to sail in an easterly direction along the coast line but has made little progress because of very strong headwinds. He adds that many of the Spaniards are ill, almost everyone is discouraged, and some are even demanding that the fleet return to Spain.

"Are they so discouraged that they might return home?" Caonabo asks, hope in his voice.

"Perhaps the problem will solve itself," old chief Mayobanex offers, speaking for the first time. He has an island-wide reputation for successfully settling disputes.

"Could they just go away?" Caonabo asks.

"Many of them would like to return to Spain, but Admiral Columbus is still in charge, and he doesn't want any of the ships returning to Spain unless they return with gold and spices. He encourages his men with talk of great gold mines at an area known as Cibao," Rodrigo says.

The chiefs look at each other, and agree they've never heard of a place or area known as Cibao. No one knows of gold mines either.

"Columbus has heard that there are vast amounts of gold at Cibao, and they want desperately to find Cibao," Rodrigo adds.

"Is gold why the invaders have come here?" asks Mayobanex.

"Not the official reason, although hunger for gold is the real reason most of the Spaniards came," Rodrigo answers. "Saving souls is the official reason."

"Explain!" Caonabo orders.

Rodrigo tells the chiefs that Christians believe that their savior, Jesus Christ, who died and went to Heaven many hundreds of years ago will soon return to Earth, and that only those humans who have been christened in the Christian Church will be saved by Jesus and given eternal life.

"What he says is true," says Chief Guacanagari, his voice rising. "Admiral Columbus explained that he can—through his savior, Jesus Christ—save our souls and give us eternal life in Heaven. Columbus says he talks directly to the Spaniards One God, and he knows all of this to be true. I believe him. That's why I was—and am—opposed to us killing the Spaniards. They can bring us salvation and eternal life! Columbus talks to God, and he is God's messenger!"

The room is silent for several moments before Caonabo says, "I am afraid what my friend Guacanagari says is not true. We have found that the invaders don't bring us salvation. They steal and rape."

"And mutilate and murder!" adds Anacaona defiantly.

Guacanagari and Caonabo stare at each other in silence until old Chief Higuayo asks: "What are Columbus' orders from his king and queen?"

Rodrigo answers that Queen Isabela and King Ferdinand issued formal instructions to Admiral Columbus. "They declared the prime objective of Columbus' voyage was the conversion of the natives to Christianity."

"That's very different than rape and murder," Guacanagari says, almost triumphantly.

"Further," Rodrigo adds, "the King and Queen ordered that the natives should be 'treated very well and lovingly'. They ordered Columbus to promote friendly relations between the Spaniards and the natives, and to punish any Spaniard who mistreats the natives."

Guacanagari smiles broadly and nods his head in satisfaction, looking in all directions. "I am not wrong to trust Admiral Columbus—and his king and queen. We can live in peace! And be given eternal life!"

Caonabo seems deflated, but quietly asks Rodrigo, "Do you believe we can trust the Spanish"

Rodrigo doesn't answer immediately. He looks at me, and I nod for him to answer.

"My father was the leader of our community, the Jews of Seville. The Spanish, at first, made many promises to us—of safety and security. My father thought he could reason with the Spanish authorities and their Inquisitors. He thought the law was on his side, and that was all that mattered."

"What did your father find out?" Anacaona asks.

"That the Spanish cannot be trusted," Rodrigo says quietly.

"What are the chances," asks old chief Higuayo, "that they don't find gold, are hungry and sick, and become so discouraged that they just leave here and return home, never to return?"

"Or if we kill them all? Will others follow?" asks Caonabo.

"More will follow, no matter what," Rodrigo says after a pause. "There are two great sea powers in Europe. The Pope has given one of them, Portugal, a monopoly to sail around Africa to India, China, Japan and the Spice Islands. Now the pope has given Spain—Castile, to be precise—a monopoly to sail across the Atlantic to India, China, Japan and the Spice Islands. The pope says the Spanish own every land they discover that is not controlled by a Christian prince."

"Who is this pope?" asks Anacaona angrily. "How can he give our lands away?"

"The pope is supposedly the infallible representative of God on Earth. He makes rules that cannot be challenged by anyone without fear of eternal damnation."

"We've never heard of this pope," says Caonabo. "What he says means nothing to us here on this island."

"But it will—and does—matter," Rodrigo says, sadness in his voice. "The pope—his name is Rodrigo Borgia—has issued three documents—they are officially called *Inter caetera* bulls—that give Spain ownership of this island and control of the people on it."

"What!" demands Caonabo.

"The pope's order," Rodrigo answers, "grants Castile all islands and mainland whatsoever, found and to be found, that are or may be or may seem to be in the route of navigation or travel…toward India."

Rodrigo looks at the disbelieving chiefs, pauses and adds, "The pope says Spain is to claim ownership of any lands not already ruled by a Christian prince."

"There are no Christian princes here because we've never before heard of the Christian church," Anacaona says, virtually spitting out the words.

After a pause, Rodrigo holds up his right hand to signal he has more. The chiefs fall silent.

"The pope also ordered the Spanish to convert non-Christians to the Catholic faith. The pope ordered that 'the Catholic faith and the Christian religion be exalted and be everywhere increased and spread, that the health of souls be cared for, and that barbarous nations be overthrown and brought to the faith…'"

Anacaona rises and declares, "There are many of us, and few of them. We must drive them and their pope from our land!"

"But it is wrong to kill!" answers Guacanagari. "The Spanish bring us the promise of eternal life. Their One God is powerful, and we should allow our souls to be saved!"

The Chiefs' Council ends near sunset without agreement. Caonabo promises to kill all Spaniards who come into his territory, while Guacanagari promises to remain friends with Columbus.

The other chiefs are undecided, except for my uncle, Behecchio, whose village is far from the Spanish fleet. He says he will prepare for the worst.

"How will we do that?" my father asks.

"We will go high into the mountains and look for places to move our women and children," my uncle answers. "We can hide for years in the mountains. The Spaniards will not go there."

"Unless," I say, "they think there is gold in the mountains."

Rodrigo says glumly, "The problem is Columbus claims there is gold everywhere."

Chapter 8
Scouting

Caonabo wants to know more about Columbus' movements and orders Rodrigo and me to return to scout the Spaniards and report back to him.

As Chief Mayobanex's village is close to the eastern edge of the island—where the Spanish fleet was last seen—we decide to travel with Mayobanex on his trip home. He welcomes our company, and we welcome his, as he is known as the wisest chief on the island.

At the last minute, to our surprise and delight, Caonabo decides to join us.

"I want to see for my own eyes," he says.

We four walk through a beautiful valley between mountain ranges. The soil is dark and rich, and our path takes us through towering mahogany, silk-cotton, and ebony trees. Little streams of water flow everywhere from the surrounding mountains. Brightly colored parrots scream at us from the trees. Mockingbirds serenade us when we camp at night.

I'm glad to be home.

Mayobanex and Caonabo are well-known and respected, and everywhere we go we are treated as honored guests. All want to hear about Caonabo's battles with the Spanish, and all are curious to look at Rodrigo, the first Spaniard most of them have seen up close. And, everyone wants to hear about my adventures in Spain.

Caonabo is fascinated by Rodrigo, and treats him with growing friendship.

As they walk briskly side by side up a steep path that skirts a mountain, Caonabo asks Rodrigo, "Columbus is a friend of yours? How can you be friendly with any Spaniard after what they did to your father?"

Rodrigo explains that Columbus is not a Spaniard. He is from an impoverished family in Genoa, which is a country not part of Spain. When he was at the royal court, he was always treated as an outsider by the Spanish at court.

"Most of the Spaniards on his fleet talk disrespectfully about him just because he isn't Spanish," Rodrigo adds.

"Why did he go to the Spanish court, if they treat him so badly?" Caonabo asks.

Rodrigo explains that Columbus spent many years unsuccessfully trying to get the King of Portugal to pay for ships to sail west to reach the east—into the Atlantic Ocean to reach India, China and the Spice Islands. The King of Portugal and his advisers studied Columbus' plans and said they were foolhardy and full of miscalculations. So, after many years of frustration—and after his Portuguese wife died—Columbus took his plans to Spain, where he again met ridicule and rejection for many years.

"The Spanish caste system is very strong and rigid, and the men of the fleet don't like being under a foreigner's command," Rodrigo adds.

"How then does he maintain his command?" Caonabo asks, bewildered.

"Queen Isabela is a strong supporter—and she is the most important person in Spain," he says. "Columbus rules in the name of the queen, and none dare—publicly, at least—to challenge the admiral."

"How did you become Columbus' friend?" Caonabo asks.

Rodrigo explains that Jews were banished from the city of Seville and the province of Andalusia in 1483. That's when his father disappeared into the Inquisition's castle.

"My mother, sister and I—I was nine years old at the time—had to leave Seville with all the other Jews after my father disappeared into the Inquisition's castle. We were taken in by a rich Jew, the Rabbi Isaac Abravanel, who lived near the Portuguese border."

He adds that Rabbi Abravanel was appointed by the queen to be a royal tax collector, a job that required him to travel with Queen Isabela's court, which has no permanent capital.

"Rabbi Abravanel made me his ward and student, so I, too, traveled with the queen's court all through Castile and Leon and Aragon. Columbus traveled with the court, as did I. As a Jew, I was an outsider. As a commoner from Genoa, he was an outsider. We were excluded from many royal social events, so we ended up spending time together."

"And you liked him?"

"Columbus is a very educated, self-taught man, and I was fascinated by his theories about sailing west to reach the east. He is a great sailor. He is very charismatic, which is what may have attracted Queen Isabela to his cause."

"The queen is attracted to Columbus?" the chief asks.

"Some at court gossip that she is overly attracted to him, but I believe she is mostly interested in his plans, which include spreading Christianity."

"How did you come to sail with Columbus?" Caonabo asks.

"1492 was a very important year in Spain," Rodrigo answers. "After 700 years of a war between Christianity and Islam on the Iberian Peninsula, the Christians—led by Queen Isabela and King Ferdinand—defeated Islam at Granada. This was a great victory for Christianity, and the religious leaders said the victory portended the long-expected Second Coming of the Christians' Savior, Jesus Christ."

"Rodrigo adds part of the reason Queen Isabela funded Columbus' voyage was to spread the word that the Second Coming of Christ was near, and—in preparation—to save the souls of infidels."

"Infidels?"

Rodrigo laughs and says: "People like yourself who are unaware of Jesus Christ or who believe in other gods."

"Is this Second Coming certain to happen?" Caonabo asks.

"Not everyone believes it. Jews believe in the same God as do Christians, but we don't believe Jesus Christ is our savior," Rodrigo says. "That's what gets us into trouble. Some Christians blame us for Jesus' death, and call us 'killers of Christ'. So, also in 1492, at the Inquisition's insistence—in preparation for the Second Coming—Jews were banned from all of Castile, Leon and Aragon."

Caonabo shakes his head, either in disbelief or confusion, or both.

"When Jews were banned from Spain in 1492, my mother and sister fled to Italy in a group led by Rabbi Abravanel. At the same time, Columbus got funding from Queen Isabela to make his voyage. I didn't want to go to Italy, and I wanted a great adventure, so I signed up to sail with Columbus."

"Where is your home now?" Caonabo asks.

After a pause and a grim smile, Rodrigo answers: "I am a man without a country."

Caonabo is silent for many minutes, before he draws near to Rodrigo and says, "Perhaps you will make this land your home."

Rodrigo smiles and says, "Perhaps."

Rodrigo tells me later, "I didn't have the heart to tell Caonabo that the Spanish believe they own this land. Jews are banned here, too."

"You can help us drive the Spanish away," I say, "and then this can be your home."

Chapter 9
Caonabo's Gamble

3 January 1494

We find everyone in a state of excitement when, after a five-day cross-island journey, we reach Mayobanex's village late in the afternoon.

His village sits near a bluff that overlooks the Atlantic Ocean, a vantage point that allows us to clearly see the Spanish fleet, anchored in the lee of a wooded peninsula that blocks the prevailing easterly winds.

Later, Caonabo, Mayobanex, Rodrigo and I gather inside Mayobanex's *bohio* to meet with several lesser chiefs. They tell us it appears that the Spanish are building a fortress and settlement on the beach just a few miles from Mayobanex's village.

No one is happy at the prospect, most especially Chief Mayobanex. "That is a bad place," he mutters.

Caonabo and I—wearing just loin clothes and painted faces—are treated as welcome and respected visitors. Not so Rodrigo. Several Taínos look suspiciously at him, dressed like a Spanish seaman.

Caonabo quickly puts their suspicions to rest by putting an arm around Rodrigo and saying, "He is my friend."

"And mine," I add.

"And mine," adds Mayobanex in a commanding voice.

"Rodrigo has even more reason to hate the Spaniards than we do," Caonabo adds. "They killed his father and banished all his people. He befriended the Taínos who were kidnapped and taken to Spain." Caonabo points at me and says, "He helped Guacocuya return home safely."

Hearing Caonabo's words, all nod assent to Rodrigo's presence. Banished from Spain, I hope silently that my friend will gain acceptance here, and want to stay.

For the next several days, we watch Spaniards unload their ships and bring ashore food, livestock—horses, cows, pigs and chickens—and cannon. To my amusement, Caonabo and Mayobanex are astonished to see the livestock. I remember my fear the first time I saw horses. Now what I fear most are the cannons—and the knowledge that the horses can be covered in armor and used as weapons. I don't tell my friends that I've seen Spanish war dogs tear a man to pieces.

"The Spaniards have sent messengers to my village asking that we visit," Mayobanex says two days later. "They are asking for help with food, and information about gold."

We discuss at length before deciding that Mayobanex and I should go to the new Spanish village—Mayobanex because he's the local chief, and me because I understand Spanish. It's agreed that dressed as a Taino it's unlikely that I'll be recognized. Rodrigo will join us, explaining—if necessary—that he had been scouting the island, as Columbus had ordered him to do.

We think the matter is settled when—to our dismay—Caonabo says, "I want to go. I want to meet Columbus."

We're shocked.

"All Spaniards know it was Caonabo who destroyed the fortress at La *Navidad*, and killed the Spaniards," Rodrigo warns. "They would love to capture you and make an example of you by burning you alive."

"How do they know it was me who destroyed *Navidad*?" Caonabo asks.

"Guacanagari told them when they came to his village," I answer.

"Guacanagari said most of the Taínos want to be friends with the Spaniards, but not you," Rodrigo adds.

"I am beginning to wonder about my friendship with Guacanagari," Caonabo says, shaking his head.

"So, you agree it's too dangerous for you to visit the Spaniards' village?" Mayobanex asks.

"It should be safe for Mayobanex to go—he has been asked to go—but I don't think it is wise for Caonabo to go," I say before Caonabo can answer.

But Caonabo just laughs and says, "There are many things I do that are not wise."

Mayobanex, Rodrigo and I all renew our protests, but Caonabo stops us. "If Rodrigo tells Columbus we are 'good Indians', will we be safe?"

Rodrigo says, "Maybe. They don't know what you look like. And they need Taínos to help them with food and water, and their search for gold. We must not ever mention the name Caonabo!"

Caonabo laughs and says, "So it's decided. We shall go to the Spanish village, and I will get to meet the great admiral. And he will meet me—but not know it!"

I have a vision the four of us burning at the stake, but I remain silent.

The next day, the four of us walk to the beach near where the Spanish fleet is moored.

Rodrigo plans to identify Mayobanex as the Taíno chief in the area, which is true. Rodrigo will say that Caonabo and I are friends of Mayobanex, but he won't even identify us by name. Only Mayobanex will talk, using Rodrigo as an interpreter.

My ability to speak Spanish will remain hidden. Rodrigo is concerned that I might be recognized, but I will go dressed only in a loin cloth with my face fully painted.

Mayobanex, Rodrigo and I are nervous, but if Caonabo is concerned he hides behind his easy-going joking nature.

As we near the beach, the first Spaniard we identify is Dr. Chanca, who I halfway trust because he didn't reveal to the Spaniards that Chief Guacanagari was lying about his wound.

"Rodrigo, glad to see you!" he says. "Where have you been?"

"The admiral asked me to scout the island." Rodrigo points to Mayobanex and identifies him as the major chief in the area. He says casually that Caonabo and I are friends of the chief.

"Didn't I meet this one at Guacanagari's village?" the doctor asks, pointing at me. I try not to show my surprise at being recognized.

"You have a good memory," Rodrigo says, quickly covering his alarm. "Yes, he has been guiding me. I have found many of the natives to be helpful."

"Well, we need help," the doctor says.

"Problems?"

"Plenty." Chanca lowers his voice and says, "Half the men are sick, and the other half want a mutiny. If everyone was healthy, we would have a mutiny."

"Are you planning on staying at this site?" Rodrigo asks.

"Because of contrary winds it took more time to sail thirty leagues from *Navidad* than to come all the way from Castile," Chanca says. "The admiral would like to go further, but so many men are sick that Columbus decided to make this place the new capital. If we hadn't stopped, I think there would have been a mutiny. Columbus is now saying that God guided us to this spot."

"The new village will be built here?" Rodrigo asks.

"Yes. Columbus says we will call it *Isabela* in honor of the queen. Maybe the name will keep her from being angry that we haven't sent gold back to Spain yet. Any ship returning home now will carry no gold—just complaints."

When Rodrigo tells Mayobanex that the Spanish plan to build a city on this spot, the chief looks surprised.

"Many mosquitos," Mayobanex says. "No good fishing. No fresh water. Nothing to block the big storms when they come out of the north."

"What did he say?" Chanca asks Rodrigo.

"He said there are better places to build. He said there are many bugs and high north winds."

"For now, we aren't going any place," Chanca says with a frown. "I've got more than 500 sick men, mostly from seasickness and dysentery. We're going to have to stay here for a while."

We see men sprawled everywhere, some under makeshift shade, others just lying unprotected from the midday sun.

We spot a small boat coming ashore from the flagship. As the boat draws close to the beach we recognize Columbus, and we walk through the sand to greet him.

"Rodrigo, my friend!" Columbus calls out loudly. He hops out of the boat, and spreads his arms.

"Isn't this beautiful?" he asks without waiting for an answer. "We will make this a great European-style city with wide boulevards, gardens, squares, grand buildings and a fortress that will protect the sea lanes, and the ships laden with gold that we will send home to Queen Isabela. God has told me this is the right place." He makes no mention of the fierce headwinds, the men's sicknesses, or hints of mutiny.

He walks for a bit and says, "Here we will build a great church, perhaps even a cathedral. We soon will begin building a royal palace so the queen can visit!"

"A royal palace? Where the queen can visit?" Rodrigo asks in disbelief. Columbus seems not to notice Rodrigo's surprise.

"Yes. A palace fit for the entire royal court."

"The queen, and the king, and the royal court? Here?" Rodrigo asks, again in disbelief that Columbus doesn't seem to recognize or chooses to ignore.

"Of course, we have much work to do, but we will get started as soon as we find the mines at Ciabo!" Columbus says with exuberance.

All I see is a desolate beach with hundreds of sick men sprawled everywhere. Mosquitos swarm.

Rodrigo introduces Mayobanex as the 'most important local chief'. He doesn't introduce Caonabo or me, and Columbus ignores us.

But he bows deeply to Mayobanex. "So, you are the King of Cibao?"

"Cibao?" Rodrigo asks, hearing the term from Columbus for a second time.

"Yes. I have learned that Cibao—the home of vast gold mines—is near," Columbus says. He adds that he has already sent Alonso de Hojeda to lead an exploratory trip to find the best routes to the gold fields of Cibao.

Columbus looks at Mayobanex, and says: "Now that King Bayernext is here, he can help us find the gold fields."

"His name is Mayobanex—not Bayernext," Rodrigo corrects quietly. "He is one of the six major chiefs of the island."

As Columbus finishes the tour of his projected new capital we are constantly attacked by mosquitos.

Rodrigo tells Columbus that Mayobanex's people have avoided settling on this spot because the nearby marshes and swamp produce so many mosquitos, and because the nearest fresh water is a mile away. He adds that there is no protection from the north winds.

"We will simply build a canal to bring fresh water here," Columbus counters. "God has told me that this is where our capital should be. And it's near the gold fields of Cibao!"

Rodrigo decides it's no use arguing with both Columbus and God about gold and mosquitos, so we say good-bye and gladly start back to Mayobanex's village.

We are relieved that Caonabo is leaving undetected, and that I wasn't recognized.

As we climb the bluff out of the new Spanish settlement, Rodrigo looks back, and says: "I've got to stay and help Dr. Chanca. He's got too many sick men to treat all by himself."

He turns and begins walking back to the new Spanish village.

As we watch Rodrigo leave us, I explain to Caonabo and Mayobanex that Rodrigo has been trained in medicine.

"You have quite a friend," Caonabo says. "He's going to help men who have done him great wrong."

Yes, I agree. Rodrigo is a great friend.

"Personally," Caonabo says with a jaunty smile, "I hope they all die of disease and mosquito bites—so I don't have to kill them."

Chapter 10
Spanish Daggers

We are in for a surprise when we return to Mayobanex's village. Caonabo's beautiful wife and daughter—Anacaona and Mencia—are waiting for us.

"I wanted to keep an eye on you, you do so many dangerous—sometimes foolish—things," a smiling Anacaona tells her husband.

"He does indeed!" laughs Mayobanex. "Your husband insisted on meeting Admiral Columbus! We couldn't talk him out of his foolishness."

"Are you mad?" Anacaona demands of Caonabo. "Don't the Spanish know it was you who attacked and destroyed *Navidad?*"

Caonabo laughs and says, "Yes, Guacanagari told them."

"That old fool is going to get you—get all of us—killed!" Anacaona says angrily.

"The Spaniards had no way of knowing who he is," I say. "Rodrigo did all the talking. He introduced Mayobanex as the local chief, but didn't introduce us, and Columbus didn't pay any attention to us. He didn't recognize even me—the queen's godson!"

Anacaona shakes her head and says, "I still say going there was foolhardy!"

"Yes, but we made it back safely," Caonabo says. "And it was worth the risk! I understand the Spanish better."

"Where is Rodrigo?" Anacaona asks suspiciously.

We tell her he stayed back to help treat the many sick Spaniards.

"How do we know he won't tell Columbus who you really were?" Anacaona asks, angering me.

"He would never do that!" I say, almost shouting.

"He's right," Caonabo agrees. "I'm certain we can trust him."

Anacaona shakes her head in disbelief. "I'm not sure I can trust your judgment after what you just did."

Trying to change the subject, Caonabo pulls his daughter to him and gives her a great hug.

"Father, you are the bravest man on the island," Mencia says. Her voice is gentle, almost worshipful.

She is—as Guacanagari said—even more beautiful than her mother. Both have long black hair and slim, curved bodies.

Our eyes meet, and Mencia smiles. I'm dumbstruck.

Mayobanex guides us to a guest hut that Caonabo, Anacaona, Mencia and I will share.

After we eat an evening meal, Caonabo surprises me by saying: "I want my wife to return the robe you gave her."

I'm startled.

Caonabo continues, "The robe is beautiful, but it is not appropriate for a man to give another man's wife such a gift, no matter the circumstances."

His eyes show friendship—but firmness.

To my dismay, Anacaona hands me the silk robe. I remember how beautiful she looked wearing it.

"But I have no use for this," I argue.

"I must give the robe back to you," Anacaona says. "It is most beautiful, but I am another man's wife."

I look down at the ground.

"It would be appropriate," Anacaona continues, smiling, "to give this treasure to an unmarried woman, if you want to."

Mencia's and my eyes meet. She smiles again. So, do I.

Delighted, I look to Caonabo, and ask, "Do I have your permission to give this to your daughter?"

"That would be most appropriate," Caonabo says, smiling. "My daughter listened to all the stories you told when we were in my village. She was enchanted. She talks non-stop about your adventures."

Enchanted?

So am I.

"This was a robe make of silk for the youngest daughter of Queen Isabela and King Ferdinand," I say, looking into Mencia's big black eyes. "The princess who once wore this robe is supposed to one day marry the King of England."

She smiles.

I hand her the robe. "This treasure is now yours."

She gives me a glorious smile. After a moment, I see that her parents also are smiling.

"Now," Caonabo says, "we have a gift for you."

From a small pouch, he carries around his waist, he pulls out a beautiful dagger with an exquisite blade and a jade handle.

I look at it in awe. "Where did you get that?"

"I took it off a Spaniard I killed."

He hands it to me. It has a herringbone and braid pattern.

It has a strong, sharp blade, and beautiful handle.

As I cradle the dagger in my hands, Caonabo says, "We have three, all taken from Spaniards we killed."

He talks about the deaths casually. I try to read his eyes without staring at him.

"I kept one of the weapons," he adds, "and Anacaona has the one she took from a Spaniard who tried to rape her." I remember—she threatened me with it!

"Now I give you the third—and most beautiful—dagger," Caonabo says. "I took it from a Spaniard who tried to steal my daughter. As a sign of respect and friendship—and because you gave my daughter a special gift."

I don't know what to say, but I take the gift as a great prize, and compliment.

I realize I've received precious gifts from queens, counts and princes, but nothing means as much to me as this blood-stained dagger.

Chapter 11
Cueno's Brag

25 January 1494

Village of Mayobanex

Rodrigo appears at Mayobanex's village shortly after noon with news.

Caonabo, Anacaona, Mayobanex and I gather in Mayobanex's *bohio* to hear his report.

Rodrigo tells us that just four days after the fleet arrived at Isabela, Columbus dispatched about 30 men, led by Alonso de Hojeda, to the interior of the island in search of gold.

"Hojeda returned after traveling for over two weeks into the central valley of the island," Rodrigo tells us, "he claims he found great amount of gold in an area he called Ciabo. The natives even gave him three great nuggets of gold, and he says the Taínos promised him that the mountains contain great amounts of gold."

We look at each other in surprise and puzzlement.

I groan because I know this bodes ill for my people, the Taínos.

"The Spaniards will endure all kinds of hardship if they believe gold is near," I say. "They won't want to return to Spain."

Rodrigo nods agreement and adds, "The Spaniards are celebrating. Even the sickest of the Spaniards now have gold fever."

Mayobanex looks at Caonabo, and says, "It sounds like they went into your territory. Have you ever found much gold?"

Caonabo shakes his head, and says: "Sometimes we have found a little gold in the rivers and streams. We don't look for it."

"What does this mean?" Mayobanex asks.

"The Spaniards have stopped demanding that the fleet immediately return to Spain," Rodrigo answers. "Talk of mutiny has ended."

We looked at each other glumly. As happy as the Spaniards are, we are depressed.

We'd all hoped that the sick and disheartened invaders would give up their quest, and return to Spain.

"What else is happening at the Spanish village?" Mayobanex asks.

"Three to four hundred of the Spaniards are sick, either from seasickness or from some kind of disease they contracted on the island, likely some form of dysentery," Rodrigo says. "We are doing all we can to treat them, but we have little medicine and we don't understand how to treat the island disease. Gold fever seems the only cure to their other ills."

Rodrigo scratches himself and mutters, "There are mosquitos by the thousands down there."

"Let's hope they all die," Anacaona mutters. She shows her dagger and stabs into the ground.

"Anything else?" Caonabo asks.

"Columbus' plans for building the village are going badly," Rodrigo answers. "With so many men sick, there aren't enough to work on the construction. The *hidalgos*—members of Spanish royalty—are balking at the idea of doing manual work—they say it is a matter of honor that they not do manual labor. So little progress is being made. They have little fresh water, but many mosquitos."

"I warned Columbus there's no fresh water where they are building their village," Mayobanex mutters.

"Columbus told me to ask you for help," Rodrigo says.

We all look at each other.

I'm certain Anacaona doesn't want to help the invaders. She stabs her dagger into the ground again.

Caonabo looks to Rodrigo, and asks: "What do you think? Should we offer them help? Can we live side by side? I doubt it, but if there's any chance…"

Rodrigo pauses before answering. He reaches into a pocket and pulls out a folded document.

"I'm not certain I should show this to you, but I think you need to see it so you'll better understand the people you are dealing with."

Rodrigo unfolds the document. "This is a copy of a letter that one of Columbus' friends—an Italian nobleman named Michael de Cueno—wrote and is sending home to friends. I can't, or won't, tell you how I got a copy, but I will read it and translate it. It was written while we were sailing near an island just east of here."

Rodrigo stands, unfolds the letter and reads:

While I was in a boat (near Santa Cruz), I captured a very beautiful Carib woman, whom the Admiral gave to me, and with whom, having taken her into my cabin (on the flagship), she being naked according to their custom, I conceived desire to take pleasure. I wanted to put my desire into execution but she did not want it and treated me with her finger nails in such a manner that I wish I had not begun. But seeing that—to tell you the end of it all—I took a rope and thrashed her well, for which she raised such unheard-of screams that you would not have believed your ears. Finally, we came to an agreement in such manner that I can tell you that she seemed to have been brought up in a school of harlots.

We're all shocked.

"Columbus gave him the woman?" Anacaona asks. "And no one on the ship—including Columbus—did anything despite the screams of the woman?"

"No one tried to stop him," Rodrigo says. "Guarocuya and I were on another ship far way, so we knew nothing about this—not until I was given a copy of this letter."

"Why is he is sending this letter to friends in Europe?" I ask.

"He is bragging," Rodrigo answers.

Anacaona pulls out her dagger.

"Help me find this man," she tells us, "so I can tame him permanently."

She slashes her dagger violently, a sidewise motion.

We know what she means.

Cueno's letter shocks me so much that I don't sleep well that night.

Well before dawn, I rise and walk toward the bluff that overlooks the sea and peer down at the new Spanish settlement. I can't fight off a sense of doom. Are my people to be enslaved? Raped? Mutilated? Annihilated?

Rodrigo follows me.

"What's wrong?"

"What's wrong, you ask? Everything!"

"Cueno's letter?" he asks. "I shouldn't have shown it to you!"

"Yes, you should have!" I answer. "The letter tells us everything we need to know about the Spaniards—and about Columbus! Columbus gave that woman to his friend Cueno. She tried to fight him off. She 'raised such unheard screams' but no one on the ship did anything to stop him. He raped her aboard the ship and no one—Columbus or any of the so-called holy men—stopped him. And then he brags about it."

Rodrigo grimaces. "It is terrible."

"That letter shows that in the Spanish eyes—and they have the blessing of their almighty pope—we have no human rights."

Chapter 12
Blades from Toledo

Later that morning, Rodrigo stares at Anacaona.

"Where did you get that dagger?"

She shrugs but says nothing.

Caonabo pulls out his dagger and shows it to Rodrigo, whose jaw drops in surprise.

"May I see them," Rodrigo asks, but both Caonabo and Anacaona pull the daggers away.

I pull out the dagger Caonabo gave me.

"A third one?" Rodrigo asks, even more astonished. "You have one, too?"

I hand mine to him, and he examines it carefully. He runs it lightly across a finger, drawing a drop of blood.

He whistles softly before saying, "This is a rare blade that likely was made in the famous steel furnaces in Toledo, in the heart of Castile."

Rodrigo looks at the chief, and Caonabo hands him his dagger.

"This, too, must have come from the steel furnaces in Toledo. It is very valuable. Kings and noblemen from all across Europe and Asia have ordered blades from Toledo to arm their soldiers. It is said that Hannibal used swords from Toledo to defeat the allies of the Roman Empire."

"Hannibal?" I ask.

"A Phoenician general and one of the great military minds of all time. Many years ago," he says.

He looks at Anacaona, and asks: "May I see yours?"

She looks at her husband who nods, and she grudgingly hands Rodrigo her dagger.

"This also looks to be made of Toledo steel, which is said to be a secret combination of wrought iron and cast iron."

"They are sharp," Caonabo says. "Sharper than anything we've ever seen."

Rodrigo laughs and sucks the blood from his finger. "Yes, they are very sharp, and strong. They also are very expensive and usually owned only by kings and generals and members of Spanish royalty—they call themselves *hidalgos.*"

"Were the men at the *Navidad* fortress *hidalgos?*" Caonabo asks.

"Obviously, some were," Rodrigo answers.

He pauses before asking, "When did you take these?"

"After they tried to kill me with them," Caonabo answers.

"But they didn't kill you."

"I killed them first. That's why I'm still here. Anacaona took one from another Spaniard."

Rodrigo looks at her with a bit of awe.

I remember seeing the charred bodies of the Spaniards at *Navidad.* None of their possessions was found.

"As a friend," Rodrigo tells Caonabo, "I should warn you that if any Spaniards see you with these weapons, you will be in grave danger."

Caonabo laughs.

"If a Spaniard sees me with this weapon, he will be in grave danger!"

Anacaona smiles and adds, "I am ready and willing to use my weapon as well."

Rodrigo starts to move his mouth, but stops before any words come out.

He hands the daggers back.

Caonabo looks at Rodrigo and asks, "Do you own any weapons like this?"

"No. I've never owned a weapon of any kind in my life."

"Never?"

"No. I doubt there were any weapons anywhere in the Jewish section of Seville, the city where I first lived, or in any of the Jewish communities I visited," Rodrigo adds.

"Jews carried no weapons?"

"I don't think so," Rodrigo answers. "Maybe some did, but we tried to rely on the law and courts and mutual respect—not force."

"I guess that made it easier to expel you, didn't it?"

Rodrigo doesn't answer. I wonder if he is thinking about his father who tried to fight force with reason and laws, and landed in a dungeon—or worse.

"And now you are a man without a country?"

Rodrigo shrugs.

Caonabo looks at Anacaona, then me, then Rodrigo.

"I'll make you this promise my friend," Caonabo says to Rodrigo. "The next time I kill one of the Spanish *hidalgos*, I will give his dagger to you. And I will teach you how to use it."

Chapter 13
Descent into Hell

Caonabo wants to war against the new Spanish settlement, and his wife, Anacaona, vehemently agrees. Chief Mayobanex continues to hesitate. "I want to know more before we send our men to kill and be killed," he says.

"So far, the Spanish have been pretty well-behaved, just like Guacanagari said they would be when they are under Admiral Columbus' command," adds Mayobanex.

"Don't be a fool like Guacanagari!" Anacaona hisses. "The invaders are only tame now because most of them are lying on the beach sick. When they get well, they will be just like the others—roaming the island stealing food and gold, and raping women. Remember that letter bragging about rape!"

I see heads nod in agreement.

"When they are weak is when we have the best chance to drive them into the sea!" Caonabo declares. "I can raise an army of 2,000 men within two weeks. If you do the same, Mayobanex, we likely can talk Guarionex and Behecchio into joining us, and also sending men."

"Eight or ten thousand warriors should easily defeat the invaders!" Anacaona says. Unsheathing her dagger, she adds: "I will join them!"

"But most of the Spaniards have rarely even left the beach," Mayobanex counters. "When we've talked to Admiral Columbus, he was most respectful."

Anacaona points to Rodrigo and asks, "You know them. Do you think they will remain respectful? Or will they go across the island stealing and raping?"

Rodrigo pauses before answering. "When they get better and stronger, they will come looking for gold. In addition to the gold hunters, there are many religious men among the Spaniards, and they will want to go to the Taínos and try to save souls."

"Should we fear their priests?" Mayobanex asks.

Rodrigo doesn't answer, so I talk for the first time: "Rodrigo and his people—the Jews—believe in the same God as the Christians—but still have been banished from Spain because they don't believe exactly the same way as the Christians. Another people—the Muslims—also believe in the same God as the Christians, but they have been warred against, defeated and humiliated by the Christians."

"How were they humiliated?" Mayobanex asks.

Rodrigo answers: "They were defeated in war, their crops were burned, their wells poisoned, their women raped. After the Muslims lost the final battle at Granada, they were at first told they could keep their religion and customs, but the Spanish have burned their books, forced conversions to Christianity, and made the Muslims abandon even their style of clothing."

"So, we should fear their religious men as well as the Spanish soldiers?" Caonabo asks.

I remember the Inquisition burning people alive, and religious men debating if Tainos have souls—or if we are monkeys good only as slaves.

I start to say something, but Rodrigo stops me, saying only, "Some of their religious men are wonderful, but some are dangerous."

I can't stop myself from saying, "I learned in Spain that it's the combination of the religious men and the warriors that is the most dangerous. Columbus thinks their God talks directly to him and blesses what he's doing. All the Spaniards—soldiers and priests—know that the pope has given them his blessing to own this island and every other place they 'discover'."

Everyone looks toward Rodrigo, who slowly nods agreement.

"Can we trust Admiral Columbus?" Mayobanex asks. "Guacanagari says we can. And if we can trust him, can he can keep his men under control?"

He looks again at Rodrigo for an answer.

After a pause, Rodrigo says, "Columbus is a friend of mine. I wouldn't be here if he wasn't. He has his flaws, but I think he is basically a good human being, and I think he wants to treat you and the other natives with respect. He thinks he is doing God's work. He believes he is helping you by saving your soul and giving you eternal life."

Mayobanex nods for Rodrigo to continue.

"I know that he has told Queen Isabela good things about the Taínos. He thinks it is his duty to save your souls. On a more practical front, he needs your help to obtain food and water and knowledge of the island. He believes you, the chiefs, are princes or regional kings who serve the emperor of China, or India or Japan, so he wants good relations. I think his intentions are good."

"So, we can trust Columbus?" Mayobanex asks.

Rodrigo takes a deep breath before answering, "He has good intentions, but I am reminded of the old sayings, 'Hell is full of good wishes or desires', and 'the descent into hell is easy'."

"Are we in a descent into the Christian's Hell?" Anacaona asks.

"I fear Columbus may lose control," Rodrigo says. "The powers at the Spanish court will demand that he bring back immense wealth—or be severely punished and humiliated. The men on the voyage are nothing but fortune hunters, and if Columbus cannot help them gain fortunes, they will revolt and ruin him. There already are signs of mutiny."

"Can he not resist these pressures?" Mayobanex asks.

"Columbus is a proud, ambitious man who wants great success and fame. The forces surrounding him are pushing him to do whatever it takes to succeed, including doing evil against you and all your people."

"So, we're facing a descent into the Christian's Hell," Caonabo mutters.

No one argues.

Chapter 14
Many Cannons

Each evening during the next several weeks while we wait at Mayobanex's village, Caonabo and Anacaona take long walks, leaving Mencia and me alone. Each night she delights in wearing the silk robe I gave her, and I take delight in taking if off her. My time with her makes me doubly glad I returned home.

After days of discussion, Caonabo makes up his mind, and says he will return to his village to organize an army, regardless of what the other chiefs decide to do.

To my dismay, Mencia will travel home with him and Anacaona. I will return to sleeping alone.

As they leave, Caonabo again urges Mayobanex to also raise an army, but Mayobanex says he is still uncertain, and he wants to meet with Columbus one more time before deciding on war.

At the old chief's request, Rodrigo and I agree to go with Mayobanex back to *Isabela*.

Before we part, I walk several miles with Mencia, Caonabo and Anacaona as they begin their trip home.

As Mencia and I kiss good-bye, I slip the sheathed dagger her father gave me into her hand.

"It's best that I not be carrying this weapon when I go among the Spaniards," I tell her. "And I want you have this to protect yourself."

She smiles and says, "I've seen my mother use hers. She will teach me how to use this dagger."

Mayobanex, Rodrigo and I return to *Isabela* the next day—the first day of February—to find much excitement and activity.

We search and find Dr. Chanca. He seems shrunken from overwork and hunger.

"I'm glad you're back, Rodrigo," he says. "I can use your help. Almost everyone is sick. I am tasting every fish and plant before it is eaten to make certain they aren't poisonous."

"I'm not sure that's wise, Dr. Chanca," Rodrigo says. "If you become ill, we'll all, be in big trouble. You have so many sick men to tend to."

"My load will soon be reduced. The admiral is sending 12 ships back to Spain. They will sail tomorrow under the command of Antonio de Torres."

"Why is this happening so suddenly?" Rodrigo asks.

Chanca lowers his voice, "Many of the men are sick. Your Indian friends have been generous, but their food is mostly local roots that the men don't like. We don't have a source of fresh water. Our men are not responding well to the change in diet, nor to the change in climate, nor the mosquitos."

Chanca looks around to make certain no others are listening, then continues: "The admiral fears a mutiny. The massacre at *Navidad* had a terrible impact on morale, and troublemakers are claiming the admiral is a liar and fraud. He's sending as many of the troublemakers as he can back to Spain. The ships are supposed to return as soon as possible with food, medicine and loyal men willing to work. But that will take months."

We see Columbus approaching.

Columbus bows to Mayobanex, who returns the honor. They also exchange smiles.

"Dr. Chanca was just telling me about the ships returning to Spain," Rodrigo says.

"Yes, they will carry back to Queen Isabela and King Ferdinand the wonderful news about the gold fields that we've discovered in Ciabo. My letter to the sovereigns tells about the discovery of rivers of gold."

Columbus adds, "Captain Torres will bring to court the giant nuggets that Alonso de Hojeda brought back from Ciabo. In total, the fleet will bring some 30,000 ducats worth of gold. In addition, the fleet will bring to Spain samples of spices—white cinnamon, pepper in shells like beans, white sandalwood, and sixty parrots."

Rodrigo looks to the ocean and sees several small boats loaded with natives being rowed to the ships.

"Why are you taking natives to the ships?" Rodrigo asks, alarm in his voice.

"Many of them are *canibali*—flesh-eaters who are enemies of the locals," Columbus says. "As cannibals their souls cannot be saved, so we may perhaps have them taken to the slave market in Seville. I'm curious what price they might fetch."

I'm shocked.

"Certainly, they are not all *canibali!*" Rodrigo exclaims. "The queen would not like Taínos being sent to the slave market!"

"Well, some of them are local natives who have agreed to go to Spain to learn Spanish so they can return as translators," Columbus answers.

I imagine their trip to Spain, and wonder how many will survive to return. I'm not hopeful.

"Some say the Indians are really monkeys," Columbus adds. "I'm not sure. Such intelligent monkeys would make good slaves."

Rodrigo senses my anger, and quietly warns me in Taíno: "Control your temper! Remember, he doesn't know you speak Spanish! Let's keep it that way."

I stay silent, but I want to scream: "We are not monkeys! We should not be enslaved!"

Columbus points to the fleet. "After the 12 sail, we will have only the flagship *Mariagalante,* the ship *Gallega,* and two small caravels."

He then looks directly at Rodrigo and asks: "Do you have any idea of the whereabouts of the *Nina?* I gave command of her to your friend the Count of Messina. I gave him permission to take the *Nina* on scouting missions, but we haven't seen the *Nina* for over two months."

Rodrigo shrugs.

"I think the count would be interested to know," Columbus continues in a conspiratorial tone, "that the three Inquisitors who sailed with us are returning on the ships that sail back to Spain tomorrow."

That, at least, is good news. I hate the thought of the Inquisition on my island.

"Why are they doing that?" Rodrigo asks, knowing the count has spent years hiding from the Inquisition.

"I'm not certain. Brother Pius will only say that his 'prey has escaped'."

Columbus is hailed from the beach and leaves us without saying goodbye.

Dr. Chanca tells us that Columbus has moved all the cannons from all the ships that are sailing back to Spain to the *Mariagalante* and the *Gallega*. They are all mounted and facing landward. "The two ships are now gunships."

"Why?" asks Rodrigo.

"The admiral fears an attack from the Indian Chief Caonabo," Chanca says. "He also fears a mutiny of his own men. Whippings and notching their ears may not be enough to keep the Spaniards in line."

Chapter 15
Admiral's Dilemma

Columbus turns back toward us and waves for us to join him. We walk with him slowly away from *Isabela* to an area where we can't be overheard.

"The priests and monks are the worst," Columbus begins. "After what happened at *Navidad,* they fear going anywhere near Indians—especially anyplace near Caonabo."

The admiral tells Rodrigo to ask Mayobanex if he knows Caonabo.

Rodrigo translates, and Mayobanex nods his head emphatically to indicate that, yes, he knows Caonabo.

"The chief says that Caonabo's village is many miles away on the other side of very steep mountains," Rodrigo tells Columbus.

"Ask him why Caonabo is so warlike," Columbus says.

Rodrigo knows the answer, but goes through the formalities of asking Mayobanex.

He waits for Mayobanex's answer before telling Columbus:

"Spaniards from *Navidad* stole from the Taínos, and raped their women. When Spaniards tried to rape his wife and daughter, Caonabo raised a small army and killed the Spanish and burned the fortress. Caonabo is now a hero among many of the Taínoss."

We walk a bit further with Columbus while he collects his thoughts.

Columbus tells us he is sending back to Spain more than half the 1,200 who sailed on the second voyage.

"I know many of the men will spread lies about me in Spain, and I know I have enemies at court who will believe the lies. I will have to depend on the queen's loyalty. She will know they lie."

Rodrigo nods.

"I want to travel into the mountains, to the gold fields of Ciabo," Columbus says. "That means I will have to divide my forces—some to stay here at *Isabela*, and some to go into the mountains to find gold."

Rodrigo cautions against dividing his forces, especially after shipping half of the men back to Spain.

"I have no choice. We must find gold," Columbus answers.

Rodrigo grunts.

"There's another problem," Columbus says. "I want soon to sail back to Juana—or Cuba, as the Indians call it—because I am sure it is the tip of a continent, probably India."

"So, you plan to divide your remaining forces into thirds?" Rodrigo says, looking stunned.

"We must maintain this capital, must find gold, and must reach the mainland of India."

"That could be quite dangerous. You could be vulnerable to attacks by Caonabo."

"That's why I'm offering a 1,000 *maravedi* reward for his capture. I want to ship Caonabo to Spain to stand trial for the massacre at *Navidad*."

"Ship Caonabo to Spain?" Rodrigo asks in astonishment. "In chains?"

Columbus nods. "I want him caught, locked in chains, humiliated and hanged."

Chapter 16
Horses!

Isabela is bustling with men joyfully packing their belongings to sail back to Spain.

Rodrigo writes a brief letter he wants delivered to the Count of Messina.

Dear Count,

As you know, Navidad was destroyed, and the Spaniards want revenge. We could have a massive bloodbath.

Queen Isabela wants souls saved, not massacred. I fear that only she can avert an all-out war against the Taínos. Please use your influence with her for good.

I should tell you that Brother Pius and associates are returning to Spain. I hope all is well with you and the countess.

Rodrigo reads me the letter. "Very short. Dangerous to say more."

He seals the letter with melted wax. He says he needs to find someone—preferably a friend of the count—he can trust to take the letter to the count.

Mayobanex, Rodrigo and I wander through *Isabela* until Rodrigo finds a man named Bernardo de Valencia. He hands the letter to Bernardo, who accepts the letter, saying, "I will do my best to get this to our friend."

"He may be at court, or at his estate in Messina."

The man nods, then asks: "Are you interested in buying a couple of horses?"

Both Rodrigo and I look at him with surprise. I remind myself that I'm not supposed to let anyone know that I can speak Spanish, so I walk away a short distance with Mayobanex. But I listen with interest.

Bernardo says he wanted a couple of riding horses so he paid to have them brought here.

"I love the horses too much to put them through the ordeal of another voyage," Bernardo says.

Rodrigo digs into his purse and hands Bernardo several coins. They shake hands.

Bernardo leads us to a small corral, and points to two beautiful horses, one a black stallion, the other a golden-brown mare.

I quietly explain to an astonished Mayobanex that when I was in Spain, Rodrigo taught me how to ride a horse. We rode many hundreds of miles across Castile, Catalonia, Aragon and Extremadura. "I loved my horse!" I tell him.

These two horses are larger than Sisi, but I don't think they are too big for me to ride. I've grown some, and I no longer fear horses—I love them!

Two nice saddles come with them, Bernardo says.

Bernardo strokes both horses' necks, and whispers something to each horse, and quickly walks away. I feel sad for him because I can tell he loves the horses.

We put the saddles on the horses, and Rodrigo takes a rope and leads them on foot out of *Isabela*.

Mayobanex is terrified by the horses, and follows us at a distance. But me—I can't stop smiling. I love to ride. Rodrigo lets me lead the mare. Outside the village—beyond site of the Spaniards—we climb aboard the horses, leaving a terrified Mayobanex to trail far behind us on foot.

What joy it is to ride a horse!

When we near Mayobanex's village, Rodrigo tells me to find a good place for the horses to graze, far enough away so the other Taínos aren't terrified.

"You need to take care of them tonight," he tells me.

"Happy to do so."

"Tomorrow you and I will ride to Caonabo's village."

I'm delighted at the prospect of a long ride, and—even more so—seeing Mencia.

Then I'm brought back to reality.

"We have to warn Caonabo that Columbus has posted a reward for his capture."

Chapter 17
Through the Mountains

The next day, I wake to a crisp, cool morning. My spirits are bright as I'm looking forward to riding with Rodrigo through the forests and rugged mountains to Caonabo's village—but over breakfast he tells me the bad news.

"You're going to have to go to Caonabo's village by yourself. I feel I must go back to *Isabela* and help Dr. Chanca—and I need to try to persuade Columbus to not start a war with the Taínos," Rodrigo says.

Rodrigo tells me I need to keep Caonabo from raiding *Isabela*—at least for now. "Warn Caonabo that Columbus has more than 50 cannons ready to blow up anyone who tries to attack."

We tell Mayobanex our plans, and he agrees that we should make another effort to avoid a war.

He shakes his head when Rodrigo asks if there are any members of his tribe who would dare ride one of the horses.

"No! We are terrified by the beasts," he says.

Mayobanex tells me I should bring plenty of supplies.

"Normally—if you were on foot—you could eat and sleep in any of the villages along your route. But everyone will be terrified of your horses, and likely will run away. I'd suggest you camp away from any of the villages."

We name the horses Count and Countess in honor of our friends in Spain. I will alternate riding one while leading the other horse on a rope.

"Both horses are used to carrying bigger men than you, but it's still a good idea to make sure you don't wear out the horses, especially climbing up mountain trails," Rodrigo says. "They will be going from sea level to high mountain passes."

Caonabo, Anacaona and Mencia started their trip home three days before on foot. They likely will arrive at their village in two more days. By horseback, I'll arrive at their village just one day or so after they arrive home.

I'm disappointed that Rodrigo won't be riding with me, but thoughts of being with Mencia more than make up for the disappointment. The prospect of a long horseback ride also eases my disappointment.

I leave mid-morning, riding Count, with Countess happily trailing behind on a lead rope. Rodrigo walks next to me for a short distance as I leave Mayobanex's village. Mayobanex and many other Taínos watch—from a distance—waving and calling good wishes.

We soon cross a small, gurgling creek and enter into dense woods. Mayobanex's village disappears from view. In front of me stand awe-inspiring mountains.

The spectacle of a man riding a horse will send Taínos fleeing into the woods. So, I am alone except the horses. I trust them to forge their way through rocky trails and over rugged mountain passes. Count and Countess and I are soon fast friends, and we enjoy our journey.

Our island has five major mountain ranges. To reach Caonabo's village, I will have to cross the Central Range, which includes our island's tallest mountain, *Pico Durate*, over 10,000 feet in elevation.

The solitude gives me time to think about all I've done in the last year. I've traveled two worlds that are so different. I came from living in a grass hut to living in the Queen of Castile's royal court, to returning home to my people—people who have no idea of the weapons and love for war that the Spanish possess. We have stones, slingshots, bows and arrows, while the Spanish have gunpowder, armor, war horses and military training.

We are a peaceful people, while the invaders seem to enjoy conquest. They have a religious leader—a pope—who has the power to give away our lands—and has done so.

I wonder what my life would have been if I'd accepted the queen's invitation to live with her. I could have studied under some of the great teachers of the time, learning multiple languages with access to the great books of the world. I'd have been friends with kings, princes and priests from throughout Europe. I would have worn fine silks, eaten endless foods, and been surrounded by servants.

Instead, I've come back to a world that is perhaps a thousand years behind Europe. Taínos don't have a written language, much less printing presses. We have only small buildings made of grass and thatch—and no towering cathedrals, castles or fortresses. The Christians have one all-powerful God, while we have many gods and *zemis*. We are taught to fish and farm and play games, while the Europeans learn mathematics, languages and science.

Is it possible for these two worlds—these two people—to live together? Are we Taínos destined to live on the bottom of the Spanish caste system? Will we even be allowed to live?

As I continue my reverie, a soaring peak rises in front of me. The pass through it is winding, steep, narrow and rugged. I will need to walk and lead the horses through the narrowest gaps.

If the Spanish believe there is gold in our mountains, even these peaks and narrow paths won't stop them.

Caonabo defeated the Spanish at *Navidad*. But can he possibly challenge the invaders when their cannons and war horses are ready for battle?

I look at our glorious mountains, rivers and streams and realize the pope has given all this splendor to Castile.

But it's our land, and I curse Rodrigo Borgia.

Chapter 18
War and Love

After three days of riding, I reach the outskirts of Caonabo's village. I leave the horses tied up about one-half mile away so as to not frighten the Taínos, and trot into the village.

I walk straight to the middle of the village to Caonabo's *bohio.* Mencia is the first person to recognize me, to my joy and hers.

She comes running to me, arms open, hugs me. "Guarocuya, how wonderful! We just got back yesterday!"

Caonabo exits his *bohio,* a wide smile on his face, and hugs me.

"Is there news?" he asks, leading me inside.

I quickly tell him that Columbus has dispatched most of his fleet—12 ships—and many of his men back to Spain. He has sent back most of the priests and monks, and the men most plotting mutiny. He's also sent all the gold he's collected—nuggets that have been given to the Spanish by Taínos who visited *Navidad* or were encountered by Hojeda when he went looking for a land the Spanish call Ciabo.

"So, there aren't many men left at the Spanish village?" asks Anacaona, who has joined us, along with a fierce-looking warrior named Marieni.

"And most of them are sick," I say. "Some of them are dying."

I add that Rodrigo stayed at the Spanish village to help Dr. Chanca treat the sick.

"Now may be the right time to attack them!" Caonabo says. "I've already started raising an army of 2,000 men, and if the other chiefs will join us, we can drive the Spaniards into the sea!"

Columbus, I warn him, has taken the cannon from all the ships—including those bound for Spain—and mounted them on the remaining ships. All the cannon—at least 50—are pointed toward land.

I add Columbus also has armored soldiers and war horses and dogs.

Caonabo looks glum at first, but then looks at me with a smile.

"Do you have a better plan?"

I say that Columbus believes there is a large source of gold in the place the Spaniards call Ciabo. Columbus plans to take most of his healthy men with him over the mountains to find Ciabo.

"How many men do you think he will take with him?" Caonabo asks.

"Perhaps 300 or 400 men."

Caonabo runs his hands together rapidly, smiles, and says, "So we don't need to take our army to the Spanish. They are coming to us."

Caonabo orders his war chief, Marieni, to send messengers to the other chiefs—except Guacanagari—telling them that Caonabo is once again raising an army.

"If they don't want to raise their own armies, tell them to send men to my army," he tells Marieni.

As Marieni disappears from the *bohio,* Caonabo asks, "Guarocuya, how did you get here so quickly? We just arrived less than a half day ago, and I know you went to the Spanish settlement, the opposite direction."

I smile and tell him about the horses.

"Horses travel twice as fast as people on foot! They are tied up less than one mile away."

Caonabo jumps to his feet and says, "Take me to them!"

Every Taíno I have seen is terrified around horses. Most run away when one of the 'great beasts' comes near, especially if the horse is clad in armor and is ridden by an armor-clad Spaniard.

Anacaona and Mencia are afraid to come close, and hang back about some 200 yards from Count and Countess.

But brave Caonabo shows no fear, and walks at my side as we approach the grazing horses.

"What great creatures!" he says. "You rode them over the mountains from Mayobanex's village?"

I tell him Rodrigo taught me how to ride—and care for—horses during our trip across Spain with Columbus last year.

"These horses are smart and strong, and they can be your loyal friend!" I say, thinking fondly of my horse Sisi back in Spain.

"Rodrigo taught you how to ride these creatures?" Caonabo asks, astonished.

"Yes. After I got over being terrified."

"Can you teach me?"

"Yes. The first thing you do is make friends." I pull some grass and feed it to Countess, who munches it happily.

Fearless, Caonabo pulls a large chunk of grass and, without just a bit of hesitation, offers it to Count, who cheerfully munches it.

I stroke Countess' neck. Caonabo strokes Count's neck.

Caonabo's smile is huge.

Another horse lover.

Over the next several days, Caonabo learns how to first walk the horses, then mount and ride.

To our joy, after about a week, we persuade Anacaona and Mencia to join us—Mencia riding behind me on Countess, Anacaona riding behind Caonabo on Count.

Mencia learns to feed and groom the horses. "I love taking care of them," she says.

But she will not ride either horse alone.

"The best part of riding is wrapping my arms around you," she tells me.

I do not argue.

As we await word from the other chiefs, we spend our days planning for war, our nights making love.

Chapter 19
Spy

Caonabo wants me to return to *Isabela* and find out what Columbus and the Spaniards are planning. And when.

Reluctantly, I agree. Reluctant because I've enjoyed immensely my time with Mencia, and because I know that *Isabela* is becoming increasingly toxic with disease, hunger and potential mutiny.

When I protest, Caonabo says, "Only you among us know their language. And your friend Rodrigo is there and can tell you much. In the meantime, we will make the spears and the slingshots."

When I start to protest again, Caonabo scowls at me and says, "Our fate may be in your hands!"

So, I have no choice.

Mencia wants to ride with me, at least to Mayobanex's village, but Anacaona, Caonabo and I all agree it's simply too dangerous.

So, I leave Mencia in tears as I mount Count for the trip through the forest and the high pass to Mayobanex's village, and then on to the Spanish settlement.

I leave Countess with Caonabo, who has already become an able horseman.

I reach Mayobanex's village to find that he's still undecided about joining Caonabo's war.

"The Spaniards have been good to deal with, at least lately," he says.

"They need you because they've run out of wine and sea biscuit—and their crops haven't come in yet," I answer. "That can change easily!"

"The admiral himself gave me this!" Mayobanex says, proudly showing me a large, shiny bell. "In return, I gave him a small gold nugget."

I don't tell him that the Spaniards laugh that the Taínos are willing, sometimes eager, to trade gold for trinkets.

I ask Mayobanex to send a runner to Rodrigo in *Isabela* asking him to come to Mayobanex's village. All the Taínos—except Caonabo, Anacaona and Mencia—won't go near a horse, so I need to turn Count over to Rodrigo.

Besides, I want to talk to Rodrigo before I enter *Isabela*.

Mayobanex offers to take the message to Rodrigo himself, and about three hours later, Rodrigo and Mayobanex return to Mayobanex's village.

Over a meal in the chief's *bohio* I tell them about Caonabo's war plans, and about his desire to know what Columbus and the Spaniards are planning.

"Caonabo wants you, Mayobanex, to join with him in the war," I add.

Mayobanex purses his lips, shrugs, and says, "I'm not certain yet that war is necessary. But some of my men have already left the village to join Caonabo. I let them take weapons and food."

"Life is not good in *Isabela*," Rodrigo tells us. "The admiral just put down another mutiny! Bernal Diaz de Pisa and several followers—we don't know how many there really are—were planning to capture Columbus, take command of the remaining ships, and return to Spain!"

"How were they stopped?" I ask.

"A drunken Spaniard talked too much. Columbus searched Diaz and found a letter he'd written, intended for court, trying to explain the mutiny. The letter reported that Columbus had punished Spaniards with floggings and mutilations."

"What happened to Diaz?"

"Diaz was arrested, put in chains, and locked aboard the flagship under guard."

"Who is this man Diaz?" Mayobanex asks.

"He is an important official—the royal fleet controller, appointed by the king and queen. He's in charge of tracking all the gold and other valuables gathered by the Spaniards," Rodrigo says.

"What will Columbus do with him?"

"He's going to send him back to Spain on the next home-bound ship. Diaz has many friends at court, and he likely will cause Columbus trouble for many years."

***

Rodrigo and I retrieve Count from a nearby glade, and walk the stallion into *Isabela,* which has about 200 ramshackle grass huts, and the start of foundations for more substantial buildings. Not much progress since I was last here.

"I'm supposed to spy," I remind Rodrigo.

"Let's find Dr. Chanca, and see what he knows."

Chanca is busy as always treating patients and has little time to talk.

But as we talk with him, Alonso de Hojeda walks up. I can sense Rodrigo's anger at the little man's mere presence.

"How's my Jew friend?" Hojeda asks derisively.

Before Rodrigo can answer, Chanca turns to Hojeda and says, "We all would be in much more trouble, especially the many sick men, if Rodrigo wasn't here to help me treat them. He has excellent medical training."

"That's good," Hojeda says, "because we need all the healthy men, we can to march into Ciabo and take control of the gold fields and mines I found."

Hojeda laughs and adds: "Any Indian who objects will have his ears cut off, and his nose slit!"

He shows off a fancy dagger, and I'm tempted to tell him Caonabo and his wife have already taken three such daggers away from Spaniards—dead Spaniards. But I say nothing.

"When are you going into the mountains?" Rodrigo asks.

"Wouldn't you like to know, you Indian-lover?" Hojeda says and stalks off. "Just tell your Indian friends that they'd better cooperate—or else!" He runs his dagger near his throat and makes a slashing motion.

I tell Rodrigo in Taíno, "We need to find out more."

"Let's just ask Admiral Columbus what his plans are."

We find Columbus talking to his brother, Diego, who has been put in charge of building a gristmill that will only work if the Spaniards dig a canal to the river about a mile away.

"We just don't have enough healthy—or willing men—to dig the canal," Diego is telling his brother as we approach.

They both greet us in a friendly manner.

Rodrigo re-introduces me as Chief Mayobanex's son.

"I knew he looked familiar," Columbus says. "But I really can't tell one Indian from another."

"I'm glad he's here," Columbus says, speaking to Rodrigo. "I need his father's help. We need guides to help us cross the mountains into the gold fields. I'm planning on taking 400 to 500 men in full military formation to Ciabo. We'll have close to 100 men on horseback. We're going to take at least two cannons, and all the dogs. That should be enough force to intimidate all the Indians, including that Caonabo devil!"

Rodrigo pretends to translate Columbus' words to me.

"Ask him when?" I tell Rodrigo in Taíno.

"When?" Rodrigo asks Columbus.

"Next week. But don't tell anyone. There are already too many rumors floating around *Isabela,*" Columbus answers. "Nobody can keep a secret."

Rodrigo and I walk back to Mayobanex's village.

"You're doing a great job as a spy!" he says with a chuckle. "You know exactly what your enemy is going to do, and when he's going to do it."

I laugh, too. "The admiral isn't very good about keeping his plans secret."

"What are you going to do now?"

"I will ride back and tell Caonabo what the Spanish are planning."

Rodrigo shakes his head. "Maybe you should stay with the Spanish. You're a great spy. "

We walk awhile in silence before I ask Rodrigo, "Do you think 2,000 Taínos can win a battle with 400 or 500 Spaniards?"

"Caonabo will outnumber Columbus four or five to one, but the Spaniards will have armor, muskets and cannon, dogs and horses. Every Taíno I've seen runs when he's charged by an armored man riding an armor-clad horse."

Chapter 20
Father Against Son

I am depressed and fearful. I want desperately to return to Caonabo's village to tell him what I've learned, and help him ready for battle—and to see Mencia. But Rodrigo and Mayobanex argue that I should travel with Columbus on his journey into the mountains—into Caonabo's territory.

"You've learned much in just a single day," Rodrigo says, "but you must learn more."

Mayobanex nods and adds, "We need to pick the time and place for war. Your skills can be key."

Mayobanex sends a messenger to Caonabo telling him what we have learned: that Columbus will lead a small army into the mountains in search of the gold fields of Ciabo.

"If Columbus takes 500 men into the mountains, won't that leave *Isabela* undefended—maybe we should attack *Isabela*?" I ask.

We know that more than half the Spaniards have sailed back to Spain, I reason, so there can't be many men left behind in *Isabela*—and those few are almost all sick.

Mayobanex shuffles his feet in the dirt before answering. "Caonabo's army—which probably isn't ready—would need at least a week to get here. Columbus likely will be back from the mountains before then."

Rodrigo nods agreement.

"I've let many of my men go to join Caonabo's army, so most of my best warriors are gone," the chief says. "So, we can't raise an army here, at least not now."

Rodrigo adds that the Spanish have many cannon on their ships, pointing to land and ready to defend *Isabela*.

"And we have another problem," Mayobanex says. "I have been told that Columbus has persuaded Chief Guacanagari to send his men to protect *Isabela*. More than 400 of his men will defend the Spanish settlement while Columbus marches into the mountains."

"Why would Guacanagari do such a thing?" I ask in shock. "That would be disloyal to his own people and to our gods!"

Mayobanex shrugs and purses his lips before answering. "Columbus flatters Guacanagari all the time. He calls Guacanagari King of the island, and says the rest of the chiefs—myself included—will be subservient to Guacanagari when the Spanish are in full control of the island. And, he has convinced Guacanagari that the Spanish One God is all powerful, and will give only his followers eternal life."

Rodrigo adds: "Columbus often invites Guacanagari to dine on the flagship. Every time he comes aboard, Columbus treats him like a king. He has the fifes and drums play, and all the officers have to rise and salute when Guacanagari joins the admiral for dinner. Columbus has convinced Guacanagari that the Spanish God will carry them to victory."

"We're losing an opportunity," I say quietly. "Caonabo will be furious with Guacanagari."

"Perhaps," Mayobanex says. "Guacanagari is jealous that Caonabo is the most admired chief on the island. He wants Caonabo defeated so he can become the King of Hispaniola."

Rodrigo paces before telling us: "Columbus is using a long-tested tactic of dividing and conquering. Columbus knows he's outnumbered by 10,000-to-one or more, but he can overcome that by dividing the Taínos' loyalty."

"This is all part of a strategy?" I ask Rodrigo, astonished.

"Every European soldier knows the tactic—it's the maxim *divide et impera*—and I'm sure the Spanish will use it everywhere they go as they try to conquer what they call the New World."

"Can't we talk to Guacanagari—to tell him he is only being used by the Spaniards?" I ask.

Mayobanex is silent for a moment before saying, "I have tried, but he won't listen. Even Guacanagari's son has told him he is wrong to help the Spanish."

"His son, Tuaymi?" I ask.

"You know him?" Mayobanex asks.

I nod. I remember the two of us scouting the Spaniards when they first marched ashore after they found the ashes of *Navidad*. I remember Tuaymi helping me hide my treasures in a cave.

"Tuaymi seemed to be no friend of the Spaniards," Rodrigo says, remembering his visit to Guacanagari's village.

"He's not. He's angry at his father," Mayobanex says, shaking his head.

"How angry?" Rodrigo asks.

"Tuaymi has left Guacanagari's village to join Caonabo's army," Mayobanex says.

We are truly divided. Friend against friend.

Father against son.

Chapter 21
Symbol of Love

12 March 1494

Village of Isabela

Columbus is angry.

He's ordered his men to line up in military formation with drums and fifes playing and royal banners flying. But instead of rigid military order and discipline, there is chaos.

Most of the trained drummers are sick or on ships headed back to Spain, and their substitutes simply can't keep time. They mostly just try to make more noise than the next drummer. The fife players are little better, and seem to know their poor playing annoys the admiral. His annoyance pleases the drummers. It's a mutiny of bad musicians.

Instead of military spit and polish, the men's clothes—after months away from home and with no women to mend them—are tattered, sickly, patched and mismatched.

"Silence!" Columbus orders, and slowly, but not immediately, the drummers stop pounding and the fife players stop playing.

Few of the 500 men look happy. Many look ill. Most look mutinous.

"We have traveled a long way together," Columbus says, sitting atop a grey mule. "Today, we begin the last leg in our efforts to find gold."

At the mention of gold, the men straighten and pay some attention. Gold fever is all-powerful.

"Alonso de Hojeda recently returned from the area in the mountains known as Ciabo," Columbus says. "Alonso, tell the men what you found."

"Indeed, Lord Admiral, my men and I traveled into Ciabo, and we found the area very rich in gold," Hojeda says. "There are rivers of gold! Many of you saw the great nuggets I brought back that have been sent to Queen Isabela and King Ferdinand. I'm sure they will be pleased—but that is just the beginning."

Some of the men cheer.

"Today we go into the mountains to become rich men!" Hojeda says loudly.

More cheer, more loudly.

Columbus waits for the cheering to die before adding: "The area we will travel to is on the other side of the highest mountains on Hispaniola. But the trip will be worth the effort. The area is known as Ciabo, which in the Indian language means quarry. That means this is the area where the Indians do nothing but dig gold from some of the richest veins of gold on earth!"

He pauses for effect before adding: "I have written King Ferdinand that the mines of Cibao will produce as much gold as the iron mines of Biscay. I am certain none of us wants to disappoint King Ferdinand."

More and heartier cheering.

Mayobanex, Rodrigo and I watch in silence.

Rodrigo quietly asks us in Taíno: "Does Ciabo mean quarry?"

Mayobanex shrugs and says, "I've never heard of an area called Ciabo, and it is not our word for quarry."

"They don't know what they're talking about," I whisper in Taíno.

But they have cannons and war horses and iron spears. And a license to steal, issued by their pope.

As the ragtag Spanish army begins its trip to Ciabo—with the drums beating out of time and the fifes battling to see which can be the loudest—we join Columbus at the head of the column. Mayobanex and I are his guides, Rodrigo his translator.

Columbus leans toward Rodrigo and says, "Hojeda told me the land we're going to is the most beautiful he's ever seen. I'm hoping that in addition to the gold mines of Ciabo, our guides can help us find the lost Garden of Eden. I have a feeling it may be near. A sign that the Second Coming of Christ is near is the re-discovery of Paradise—the Garden of Eden."

We promise we'll keep our eyes open for Paradise—perhaps what we had before the Spaniards arrived.

After marching for nearly two weeks, covering about seventy miles into the mountains, Columbus tells us that he is pleased because 'all the creeks and streams, large and small, have gold nuggets. I am certain that this gold comes from the mines on the peaks and mountains, and during the rainy season the water carries it into the streams'.

He adds that some of the nuggets he's seen are 'big as walnuts'.

Rodrigo, Mayobanex and I look at each other in wonder—we have seen no gold nuggets.

Columbus decides to build a fortress on the bank of a large river on a high hill where the Spanish can protect their miners from Caonabo's warriors.

"I will name the fort Santo Tomas, the apostle and original Doubting Thomas," Columbus says. "Those of you who doubted me are being proved very wrong."

Leaving fifty Spaniards behind to explore, gather gold and build the fortress, the rest of us march back to *Isabela,* arriving on April 1, just before the Christians' Easter celebrations.

Columbus' brother, Diego, who'd been left in charge of *Isabela*, meets us and says there have been more deaths from illness and more signs of mutiny.

"I've found letters meant to go to court accusing you of cruel punishments, mismanagement, corruption and other misdeeds," Diego tells Columbus.

More bad news comes Columbus' way several weeks later.

A messenger arrives from Fort Santo Tomas.

"Lord Admiral," the messenger says, "I've come to tell you that all the Indians who were helping us build the fortress and search for gold have fled. They say they fear for their lives because an army led by the great Chief Caonabo is on its way to destroy the new Spanish fort. Caonabo is vowing to kill every Christian he finds, and any Indian who's helping us."

Columbus looks at the Spaniards who've gathered and asks: "Where is Hojeda? Tell him I need to see him."

Hojeda appears within minutes, and the messenger repeats the threats the Spaniards are facing at Santo Tomas.

"What are your orders, Lord Admiral?"

"Take 70 men immediately to the fortress and do whatever is necessary to cow the Indians into learning to obey," Columbus answers. "Bring me Caonabo in chains. I want to make an example of him. I repeat: Do whatever is necessary!"

Rodrigo and I are standing in the crowd of listeners. Columbus points to Rodrigo and tells Hojeda, "You'll need to take Rodrigo as your interpreter. And that young Indian next to him is Mayobanex's son. He'll be your guide."

Neither Rodrigo nor I want to go, especially with Hojeda in command, but we now have no choice.

Hojeda looks at us, shakes his head in disgust, and orders us to be ready to march early the next morning.

I rush to Mayobanex's village and tell him what's happening.

"Send messengers to find Caonabo and warn him. Hojeda is hunting for him."

Mayobanex agrees, then tells me Caonabo has sent me a message. He hands me a small packet, wrapped in cotton.

I open it. It is the Spanish dagger that I gave to Mencia.

I look puzzled. "The messenger said only that Caonabo's daughter thinks you need this more than she does."

I look at the dagger and wonder how a weapon of war can be such a symbol of love.

Chapter 22
Ears

I spend the night in Mayobanex's village because I need to escape—if even for one night—the Spanish settlement and its mosquitos, diseases, mutinies and floggings.

I rise early, say goodbye to Mayobanex, and trot back to *Isabela.* I'm in for a shock when I arrive.

Almost all the able-bodied Spaniards are preparing to march into Ciabo.

I rush to find Rodrigo to ask what is happening.

Even though we are talking in Taíno, Rodrigo lowers his voice to a whisper, and says, "Hojeda talked Columbus into making a show of force, so instead of just 70 men, all able-bodied men have been ordered to go with Hojeda."

"Why are you whispering?"

"Guacanagari's men began arriving last night. We need to be even more careful than ever with what we say, because there are ears—Spanish and Taíno—everywhere."

Traitors.

"How much danger is there?"

"Columbus is in a terrible rage," Rodrigo answers. "He's uncovered another attempt at mutiny. He's had one of the mutineers whipped, he cut off the ears and nose of another mutineer, and he had their leader, Gaspar Ferriz, hanged!"

"Hanged?" I ask, stunned.

"Yes. Don't go near the ships. Columbus has left him there hanging as a warning to any other mutineers. It's a horrible sight."

I am glad to leave *Isabela* later in the day after seeing a man with no nose and another without ears. I avoided seeing the hanged man. I need no reminder of how cruel the invaders can be.

Nearly 400 men accompany Hojeda, including about 75 armored men on war horses, and 20 or so vicious war dogs. Rodrigo and I stay near Hojeda in the front of the small army while the dogs—which terrorize me—trail at the back of the army.

No drums and fifes play, and no royal banners fly. This seems more like a mob seeking revenge than a royal military force.

I find myself touching the dagger I've hidden in a small pouch. It reminds me that I'm not powerless, and that I'm loved. I pray to our gods for Mencia and for Caonabo and his men.

For many hours, we see no Taínos. They have all fled at the report that both Caonabo's and Hojeda's armies are near.

An unusual silence hangs over the Spanish army—perhaps because of the mutilations and hanging at *Isabela.* Perhaps because they fear Caonabo's attack is imminent.

I feel a sense of doom. Thoughts circle in my brain that I can't stop:

War horses, war dogs.
Cannons, muskets.
Gunpowder, armor, iron spears and lances.
A thirst, hunger for revenge.
A willingness—an eagerness—to kill.
They think my people are monkeys without souls, good only as slaves.
Their pope, who speaks for their Almighty God, says they have the right to rule.
Over us. Over our lands.

I keep looking for a chance to flee into the woods. I want to join Caonabo's army. I want to unsheathe my dagger in battle. For the first time ever, I am thirsty for blood. Spanish blood.

But I can't leave my friend Rodrigo alone. He'd be punished if I escaped.

Late in the afternoon, the hair on my arms and neck stands straight up. That has never happened before.

I show the raised hairs to Rodrigo, who says, "I sense danger, too."

Horses neigh nervously, dogs bark.

But we see nothing unusual.

Hojeda reins in his horse, dismounts and calls his top lieutenants to his side.

He orders Rodrigo and me away so we can't hear what they say, but after a few minutes several horsemen ride out in different directions, apparently acting as scouts.

Hojeda orders his army to continue forward, slowly and cautiously.

We follow a narrow path along a deep river bordered by steep bluffs.

One scout horse returns—without its rider.

Then a second horse, and a third return without riders. Color drains from Hojeda's face.

Caonabo's army is near.

A fourth horse races toward us, this one with a rider that has an arrow in his side. Blood is running down the horse's side, but I can't tell if it is the horse's or the rider's blood.

Hojeda grabs the horse's reins and stops the terrified animal. The wounded rider falls off the horse and says, "We are surrounded. Maybe 2,000 Indians."

The man passes out, and Hojeda catches him and lowers him to the ground. Hojeda's hands are soaked in blood. I'm relieved that the horse is not injured.

We look up and atop the bluffs we spot Caonabo's warriors. He's picked a good spot to attack. His army has the high ground. Retreat is not an option.

Long spears begin flying through the air. Caonabo's men are launching them with slings that enable them to send the javelins faster than if they shot with bows and arrows. Rodrigo and I dive under a small cart.

Taíno warriors, painted in black and other colors, scream frightening cries. I secretly cheer.

Some of the Spaniards cower and run, but Hojeda does not panic. He stands fearlessly looking at Caonabo's army, a smile on his face.

He orders his men to form a circle. Many of the Spaniards have shields that easily deflect the javelins and rocks. Many of the horses also have armor. Surprisingly, few Spaniards are wounded.

Hojeda orders the mounted men to organize into attack formation.

"Charge!" he orders, pointing to the bluff with the least grade.

Fifty horses with men carrying massive swords charge the Taínos.

Javelins and rocks continue to bounce off the armor.

Mounted Spaniards rip into Caonabo's men. Iron swords slash through the painted bodies.

Horses trample people.

Dogs follow, chasing Taínos, chewing the wounded. Mounted warriors spear wounded, prone warriors.

The Taíno warriors flee in panic.

The mounted Spaniards turn and race up another bluff.

Taínos who don't flee die on the spot. Spaniards run spears through them time and again.

Just a few minutes have passed, but all Caonabo's men are gone.

Dead or fled.

I stand in stunned, unbelieving silence.

"It was the horses," Rodrigo whispers to me. "They were terrified of the men on horses."

"And the dogs," I answer. We see dogs chewing on corpses.

Hope is lost.

I vomit and faint. Rodrigo carries me away.

Caonabo's army is no more.

As if through a daze, I hear Hojeda order: "Capture prisoners!"

Two hours later, several mounted Spaniards return to Hojeda's army, dragging four bound, beaten Taínos behind the horses.

Hojeda knocks Rodrigo and me away when we try to try to help the Taínos.

He orders Rodrigo to question them.

"These men are from the village of Ponton," Rodrigo tells Hojeda after listening to the eldest Taíno. "This is the chief, his brother and his son. The fourth man is also from Ponton. He is just a farmer. They were not part of Caonabo's army."

Hojeda spits.

"They say they have been helping the Spanish build their fortress," Rodrigo adds. "They say they are friends of the Christians!"

"And you believe their story?" Hojeda asks derisively.

"They are not painted for war," Rodrigo says.

Hojeda notices that the Ponton chief is wearing a Spanish shirt.

"Where did you get that shirt?" he demands, and Rodrigo asks.

Rodrigo translates the answer: "The chief says three Spaniards paid his men to carry them across the river. The Spaniards took off their shirts, and left them behind. His men brought the shirts to the chief as gifts."

"Place these thieving Indians in chains!" Hojeda commands. "They have stolen from Christians. They will be punished!"

"Punished? For what?" Rodrigo demands but is ignored.

Hojeda asks the men who captured the four: "Where is this village?"

"Just a mile or so that way," one of the men says, pointing west.

Hojeda orders us—the four captives included—to march to the village, where he commands all villagers to assemble. None is painted for war.

Hojeda orders Rodrigo to translate, and Hojeda tells the villagers:

"We have defeated your army. Many of your men—Caonabo's men—are dead. Caonabo may be dead. Few Spaniards are even injured."

Villagers moan in dismay.

"Silence!" Hojeda commands, then announces: "We captured your village chief wearing clothes he stole from Christians. He and his brother and his son will be taken to Admiral Columbus for justice to be done!"

He runs his hand over his throat in a slicing motion.

"Any questions?"

Rodrigo translates in a stuttering, stunned voice.

No one dares to speak.

Hojeda orders one of the bound Taínos—the farmer—brought forward.

"Hold him good!" he tells his men.

Hojeda takes out a dagger.

He smiles at the villagers.

"You all must learn what Spanish justice is."

Hojeda slices off the man's left ear.

A horrible cry of pain is heard. From the man, from the villagers.

The man faints.

"Pick him up! Hold him good!" Hojeda orders.

With a smile on his face, he slices off his right ear.

Rodrigo tries to help the maimed Taíno, but Hojeda orders, "Hold that Jew! Cut off his ears if need be!"

No one else dares to help the maimed Taíno.

Hojeda rides his horse through the villagers, holding the ears as trophies high over his head. A great smile covers his face.

"These other three I will take back to *Isabela* for Admiral Columbus to decide their fates. I will recommend that we burn them at the stake—alive!"

As we march out of the village, the Spaniards cheer for Hojeda.

The villagers resume their moaning.

The earless man lies in a puddle of his own blood.

I look back and see Taínos rushing to help him.

Chapter 23
Jeremiah 23:1

I'm so distraught over what I've seen—the mutilation of an innocent man and the defeat of Caonabo's army—that I become sick again I want to escape and return to my people—and learn if Caonabo survives—but Rodrigo says I must stay with the Spanish army in hopes of saving the three captive Taínos.

"No one else will try to save them," he says bleakly. He, too, is pale from the maiming we've just witnessed.

Spaniards beat and kick the chained men during our descent down the mountains. After five days of miserable marching, we arrive in *Isabela*. We are ordered not to help the captives, but at great risk we smuggle water to them.

Hojeda orders his jubilant men to parade the three captives past the body of the man they hanged before we left *Isabela*. Birds are feasting on the Spaniard's corpse, which dangles from makeshift gallows. The eyes are gone, and much of the face.

"You're next! You're next!" Spaniards chant to the uncomprehending Taíno captives.

Columbus greets Hojeda like a conquering hero, bowing to the young commander.

Hojeda lies and says, "I've brought you three captives from Caonabo's defeated army, Lord Admiral."

"Glorious job, Alonso!" Columbus responds. "I will send a complete report to the sovereigns telling them of your work on behalf of our Lord and Savior!"

Hojeda bows, and all the men cheer.

"How would you like to dispose of your captives?" Columbus asks.

"I would suggest that we make an example of Indians who oppose Christianity," he answers. "I made a public example of one other captive in their own village."

"An example?" Columbus asks.

"I made the Indians in the village watch as I sliced off his ears."

Hojeda opens a small pouch and shows Columbus. "My trophies. Unless you want them, Lord Admiral."

Columbus steps back in revulsion. Realizing he'd shown weakness in front of the men, he asks again, "How should we deal with your three prisoners?"

"They could be drawn and quartered, and we could hang their body parts around the countryside as a warning to Caonabo," Hojeda suggests. "Or we could burn them at the stake. That will show the pagans who's in charge here!"

Columbus, after a pause, agrees: "Yes, make an example. We shall behead them in the public square in three days."

All the men cheer in agreement, and hats fly in the air.

Rodrigo whispers to me, "Beheading is considered one of the kindest forms of execution. Death is instant, compared to being burned to the stake, or being drawn and quartered."

His words are no consolation.

Rodrigo sees how ill I look and decides to get me out of *Isabela*.

"Go to Mayobanex. Beg him to come to *Isabela*. Maybe he can help us talk some sense into the admiral. You must come back, too."

Mayobanex is distraught when I recount what happened.

He also has some good news: Few Taínos were killed in battle because so many fled. "The horses just terrorized them."

He tells me, to my great relief, that my father, uncle and Caonabo survived. The humbled Taíno army retreated into the mountains.

I recount the maiming of the innocent Taíno at Poton. I spare telling Mayobanex that Hojeda kept the man's ears as trophies. "I don't know if he survived."

"I do know. He died in his wife's arms," the chief whispers.

I close my eyes and silently say a prayer for the butchered man.

"Rodrigo hopes you can help us talk Columbus out of killing the captives."

"Every time I go into *Isabela* I hate it more," Mayobanex says. "They whip and mutilate their own men. I have heard that they have even hanged one of their own men."

I don't tell him that man's eyeless body is still hanging as a warning to possible mutineers.

"Three innocent men will die if we don't help them," I say.

"They may die anyway, but I will try. "

As the evening breeze rises off the ocean, we search for Rodrigo once we enter *Isabela*. We find him with Dr. Chanca and Columbus' younger brother, Diego.

"We've been pleading with the admiral to free the three captives," Rodrigo says. "We have him convinced that the three were not part of Caonabo's army. Fortunately, one of the men from Fort Saint Tomas arrived, and identified the three as Taínos who had been helping the Spanish at the fort."

Mayobanex asks if he can see the three captives.

"Yes, but you won't like what you see," Diego answers.

We all walk halfway through the village to find a wooden cage, no more than four feet tall, four feet wide, four feet deep. A dog kennel. Inside are the captives, locked in irons.

The three Taínos are blood-smeared. The chief's nose is broken and bleeding.

Even as we stand there, a guard flicks a pebble at the captives.

"Why are you doing that?" Diego demands.

"It helps me pass the time," the guard answers.

"Stop it now, or I'll have you thrown in there too."

The guard shrugs.

"Take me to the admiral!" Mayobanex demands of Diego.

As we leave, we hear another pebble bounce off the caged men.

"I said stop that!" Diego says fiercely. The guard shrugs and smiles.

We find Columbus in his hut reading a Bible.

He's dressed in a simple brown robe, looking like a Franciscan monk. His once brown hair has turned pure white, and he's lost at least 20 pounds since the fleet sailed from Cadiz.

He looks up from scripture and silently waves us inside.

"I have brought our friend, Chief Mayobanex, to beg you—as I have—to free the three captives, who are known to be our friends."

Tears begin flooding down Mayobanex's cheeks.

"Many of us have tried to be your friends," a sobbing Mayobanex says, speaking through Rodrigo. "Is this how a great man treats friends?"

He goes down on his knees and clasps Columbus' hands. "I beg you to free the men who have been unjustly chained, caged and condemned."

"I remember, brother, what you wrote in your log not long ago," Diego adds. "You wrote: 'I believe that in all the world there is no better people (than the Indians). They love their neighbors as themselves, and they have the sweetest talk in the world, and are gentle and always laughing'."

"Did not the queen, your great friend Isabela, instruct you to treat the natives with 'love and kindness'?" Dr. Chanca asks.

Columbus nods, and strokes the sobbing Mayobanex's hair. Tears trickle down both men's cheeks.

"I went to see the captives," Columbus says in a ghostly voice. "I looked in their cage, and I saw myself wearing chains and people jeering at me. It frightened my soul."

The image startles us.

"I have been reading the Bible—Jeremiah 23:1" He reads aloud:

What sorrow awaits the leaders of my people—the shepherds of my sheep—for they have destroyed and scattered the very ones they were expected to care for.

Columbus stands, helps Mayobanex to his feet, and says, "I am supposed to be your shepherd. I will not destroy any more of the Lord's flock."

"What are you saying, brother?" Diego asks.

"Remove their chains, free them from their cage, take them out of *Isabela* tonight."

We stand looking at Columbus, disbelieving, until Dr. Chanca says, "You heard the admiral. Follow orders!"

Chapter 24
A Magical Gift

"Report to Admiral Columbus, immediately!" Diego tells the drowsing guard, who spits and shuffles off slowly toward the admiral's hut.

Dr. Chanca arrives with a small cart, pulled by a skinny donkey. "My dead man's cart used to haul corpses to the graveyard."

We say nothing back.

"I'll need it back," the doctor adds.

We unlocked the cage and help the three captives out, lifting them as gently as we can into the dead man's cart. This one time, fortunately, we are not going to the cemetery.

Stars and a quarter moon provide us our only light, but we guide the cart and the captives safely out of *Isabela*.

Diego motions that he's returning to *Isabela*. "There will be trouble when Hojeda learns my brother freed the prisoners! I must be there to help my brother."

We nod, wave thanks, and take the cart and the freed captives to Mayobanex's village. We carry them into a hut. Villagers, without asking, bring food and water, and nurse the three.

"Can't stay here long," Rodrigo warns Mayobanex. "Hojeda will surely search here."

"Let me worry about that," the chief says. "Tomorrow you must return to the Spanish village. We need to know what is happening. Send us warnings if you can."

We sleep fitfully in Mayobanex's village. When we wake, we watch the path to *Isabela*, fully expecting to see angry Spaniards charging up from below, but none comes.

We fill the cart with manioc, sweet potatoes, squashes and beans. Our cover story will be—if asked—that we have the cart to get food from the native village. We hope starving Spaniards won't suspect our roles in the captives' escape.

We fear the worst, but when we arrive in *Isabela* we find not anger at the captives' escape, but joy that a ship has arrived from Spain.

"The ship is full of medicine, flour, wine, rum and other food we haven't seen for weeks!" Dr. Chanca tells us when we return his death cart.

We see that most of the men are already drunk from drinking the rum, which Columbus distributed in large amounts.

"And the captives?" Rodrigo asks in a near whisper.

"Pretty much forgotten the moment the *Nina* arrived."

"The *Nina?*" Rodrigo asks, astonished.

"Yes. The trusty little caravel has returned, bringing food, medicine and hope."

"Is the Count of Messina her captain?" Rodrigo asks the doctor, hope in his voice.

"I don't know. Ask the admiral."

We hurry to Columbus' hut.

He smiles at us, "God sent the *Nina* back to me as proof that my freeing the captives was the right thing to do. God rewarded me—his shepherd—for protecting his flock. Even Hojeda agrees it's a sign from God!"

Rodrigo and I glance at each other, glad that the Spaniards won't be pursuing the freed captives.

"Was the Count of Messina aboard?" Rodrigo asks.

"No. He sent me this message:

Dear Lord Admiral,

I returned to Spain as quickly as I could, as King Ferdinand had instructed me. I apologize for not informing you. The winds were best to sail immediately.

I send the Nina back to you with thanks, and full of supplies that I'm certain you and your men will need. All is well.

I wish you and my friends the best, and hope to hear news of all of you as soon as possible."

May God be with you always.

Your friend,
The Count of Messina.

"That's all?" Rodrigo asks.

"You know the count must be careful," Columbus says. "There was a large man—a black man—aboard the *Nina* who's been looking for you. I saw him last with my brother, Diego."

"A black man?" Rodrigo asks, a rare smile highlighting his face. He says only, "Let's find Diego!"

We walk quickly to Diego's hut, knock and enter.

"Rodrigo!" shouts a big black man with a huge smile on his face.

"Hector! My friend!"

"So, you do know this strange man?" Diego asks.

"He helped raise me. As I think you know, I traveled with the royal court for many years, living with the two court rabbis, Isaac Abravenel and Abraham Senior. Hector was Rabbi Senior's servant—and friend!"

Hector nods, and adds: "I was captured in North Africa as a small boy and taken to the slave market in Seville. Rabbi Abraham bought me, and freed me. Then I worked for him for many years—until he died last year."

"I always thought of you as my older brother," Rodrigo says. Hector smiles, and says, "Thank you. I have no other family."

I remember meeting—although never actually seeing—Hector at Rabbi Abraham's deathbed in Barcelona last year. I am surprised to find him such a large man, and so much younger than I remember. He fooled me and many others then with his disguise as an old, hunched-over, deaf-mute. Now he stands straight and tall and beardless. His voice is deep and pleasant.

"How did you come to sail on the *Nina?"* Rodrigo asks.

"When the count returned to court, I was there, working for the Countess of Messina. The count said he needed to return the *Nina* to Columbus, but he couldn't sail back. He said Rodrigo was likely here. Since I have no other family, I asked him if I could sail on the *Nina."*

Rodrigo hugs Hector. "I am so glad!"

"Is it safe to talk here?" Hector asks.

Diego shakes his head. "Nowhere is safe. The walls are thin. Spies are everywhere."

"I need to tell you things in private," Hector says to Rodrigo. "No offense Diego."

"One cannot be too careful here," he answers.

The three of us walk in silence several miles down the beach. It's a beautiful day, with a breeze filtering through the pine and palm trees. Waves crash rhythmically, calming my nerves, and keeping sounds from carrying far.

We find a large rock to sit on.

Hector double-checks that no others are near.

"The count and countess have gone to their estate in Messina on the island of Sicily. It's as far from the Inquisition as they can get. But they know the inquisitors will never give up chasing him."

"You know that the Inquisition condemned both the count and his father to burn at the stake?" Rodrigo asks, surprised.

"I do. The count told me I could tell you that I am a member of the Order of Montessa—the former Templars."

Rodrigo looks surprised, but stands, and he and Hector exchange some type of hand signals.

Hector points to me, "Does he understand any of this?"

Rodrigo laughs. "I should have told you. He speaks Spanish. He's a great listener."

Hector shakes my hand, and says, "I remember you from the rabbi's death bed. Because you helped the rabbi and because you are Rodrigo's friend, I will be your friend until the day I die."

Taken aback, I pause before answering: "And I will be your friend until the day I die."

The vows of friendship warm my heart. I feel hope for the first time since Caonabo's army was defeated.

"I have something for each of you," Hector says.

He gives Rodrigo several letters—one from his mother and sister, one from Rabbi Isaac, one from Prior Perez at *la Rabida*, and one each from the count and countess.

Hector hands to me two packets.

The first is from the count—ten more large gold doubloons. "He said maybe you can buy your own ship someday," Hector says.

The second is from the countess. It is heavily wrapped in cloth, and it takes me several minutes to open it.

I can't believe what's inside.

"It's a mirror made from Venetian glass!" I exclaim. "I saw the countess look into this when she was brushing her hair. I was stunned by everything about it. I can't believe she sent this to me."

When I look in the mirror, I see a man who desperately misses his woman.

"There's a note," Hector says.

I unfold it.

Dear Guarocuya,

I hope with all my heart that this gift reaches you, and that you are well.

I remember how this mirror amazed you. It is my gift to you.

Please give it to your woman—I hope you have one! Tell her good things about me.

If you ever somehow can, send me word of your life, and of Rodrigo's.

I hope our paths cross at least once more in this life.

Always your great friend and admirer,

The Countess of Messina.

PS: the queen mentions your name often. Don't forget she is your godmother.

This has been the best day in many. The captives are free. The *Nina* is back. I have received warm wishes from friends far away. Hector and I are friends for life.

And I have a magical gift for Mencia.

Chapter 25
Tuaymi

Rodrigo asks me what I did with the first gold the count gave me.

I remember the gold coins—and the other gifts: the beautifully carved chess set from Rodrigo, the silk robe from Prince Juan, the Queen's Bible, and her ring.

"I gave Princesses Catherine's robe to Mencia," I answer. "The rest I hid in a cavern near Guacanagari's village."

"Good. How far away is the cavern?"

"It's this side of *Navidad.* Twenty or so miles."

"Let's go there," Rodrigo says.

We agree we don't want to spend any more time than we have to with all the drunken Spaniards at *Isabela.*

Hector adds that he'd like to see more of the island. "Need to get rid of my sea legs," he adds.

"I'd like to hear news of Tuaymi, Guacanagari's son," I add. "He fought with Caonabo's army." We are all anxious to hear details of the battle.

We continue walking along the beach in a westerly direction until we find a well-worn path that leads us to the top of a bluff. We meet several friendly Taínos who confirm that the trail will lead us to Guacanagari's village.

We tell Hector that Guacanagari has aligned himself with Columbus, and that Guacanagari's son sided with Caonabo.

"Mmmm. It's terrible when father fights son," Hector says.

We tell Hector that Columbus has made many promises to Guacanagari, including that he'll be the king of Hispaniola when the Spanish defeat Caonabo.

"Caonabo—who is the father of my woman—led the army that destroyed *Navidad*, and tried to battle the Spaniards at Fort St. Tomas," I say.

We add that Caonabo's army lost that battle. The other chiefs, including our friend Mayobanex, have tried to remain neutral, although they often help Caonabo, including letting their men join his army.

Tuaymi disobeyed his father and joined Caonabo's army.

"Tuaymi hates the Spanish," I say. "The Spaniards at *Navidad* stole and raped. When he tried to stop them, they cut off his right ear lobe. He thinks his father is wrong to help Columbus. I'm hoping he returned to his father's village after the battle at St. Tomas."

As we near Guacanagari's village, I note that the fields are full of women tending the crops, men are fishing in the streams, and that children are running around in the ball field—unlike my earlier visit when nearly everyone had fled from the Spaniards. I remember playing on the ball fields against my friends, and against teams from neighboring villages.

We find Guacanagari sitting in the shade outside his *bohio.*

He recognizes both me and Rodrigo from his trips to *Isabela,* but his greeting is less than warm.

"Who's this?" he demands, pointing at Hector. I realize that none of the Taínos have ever seen a black man, nor anyone as big as Hector.

"A good friend of Admiral Columbus," I answer, exaggerating.

"Then he is welcome," the chief says, motioning us inside his hut.

The inside of his *bohio* is filled with Spanish items—bells, a ship's clock, a royal banner, and other items. There's a small alter with a Madonna, and a small silver cross hangs from the chief's neck.

He sees us looking at Spanish goods, smiles and says, "I give the admiral gold and food and guides, and he gives me gives many presents—and the promise of eternal life! I have taken Jesus into my heart!"

I ask him, "Have you been baptized?"

"No, but Admiral Columbus says he will arrange it soon."

Then I ask, "Where is your son Tuaymi? I need his help."

To my shock, Guacanagari's face twists into a horrible scowl—a combination of anger, sorrow and hatred.

"Caonabo killed Tuaymi!"

"Caonabo? Killed Tuaymi?" I ask, stunned.

"Tuaymi refused to accept the Spanish God, and he went off to join Caonabo to fight for our old, weak gods. He chose Caonabo over me and over the One God, Jesus and eternal life. His soul is lost!"

I stare at the old chief's face, but can see nothing but anger and hatred.

"You said Caonabo killed Tuaymi. How?" I ask again.

"A Spanish horse ran him down and trampled him near the new Spanish fortress. But my son wouldn't have been there at all if not for Caonabo. He killed my son! Caonabo will be forever my enemy!"

I exchange glances with Rodrigo and Hector. "No use arguing with him," Rodrigo tells me in Spanish. Too much anger.

We retreat from Guacanagari's *bohio* and his anger. He does not say goodbye.

"Why was he so angry?" asks Hector, who senses the chief's fury even without understanding the Taíno language.

"His son was killed by a mounted Spaniard. But he blames not the Spanish, but Caonabo for putting him in harm's way," I answer.

We leave the village in silence.

On the outskirts, I ask a villager how to find the cavern of our gods, and he shows us the way.

"We come to pray for Tuaymi," I tell him.

"I'm sorry—very sorry—but I cannot join you," says the villager as he leaves. "We can no longer pray to our old gods. And none of us is supposed to utter beloved Tuaymi's name."

As Rodrigo and Hector bow their heads in silence, I say prayers for Tuaymi—one to the goddess Atabey, our most important god, and to Maketaori Guayaba, god of the underworld and the dead.

Then we take my treasures and flee.

Chapter 26
Hector

Rodrigo asks what I plan do with my treasures, carried in a makeshift knapsack made from my old Spanish sailor's shirt.

We agree *Isabela* is not an option—too many thieves.

"I'm going to Caonabo's village," I decide. "I want to see him. I need to see Mencia. I can leave everything there."

Rodrigo says he must return to *Isabela* because he's only one who can translate between the natives and the Spanish. "I'm trying to keep the peace."

Hector looks unsure, and says, "I didn't find much to like about *Isabela*. Too many mosquitos, too many sick people, and too many drunken Spaniards. Not a good place for a black man. I have papers proving I'm a free man, but there are always some men willing to sell me into slavery again."

"Would you want to come with me?" I ask.

Hector answers that he'd love to see more of the island—and stay far from *Isabela.*

I'm glad to have his company.

Before we part, I ask: "Rodrigo, can I give you the gold? I have no use for it. My people don't give it any special value."

Hector says the count gave me gold because 'he thinks maybe you can use the gold to ransom a friend, or maybe you can buy a ship and sail away'.

I appreciate the count's kindness, but I ask Rodrigo again to take the gold.

"No, I don't want to carry a fortune among the gold-hungry Spaniards. You'd best find another hiding place, and hope your gods can protect it."

Rodrigo gives us each a hug, and Hector and I watch him return to *Isabela.*

Hector and I then walk briskly, trying to put distance between us and Guacanagari's bitterness.

We have to cross the mountains again, but the path is well-worn, and the Taínos we meet are happy to feed us, and share their shelters. All are curious about the big black man traveling with me, but most are too polite to ask questions. Most have heard tales about my kidnapping, travels to Spain and friendship with Caonabo—so I am usually treated as a special person.

I enjoy Hector's company. At first, our talk is mostly about Rodrigo.

"Smartest, kindest person I ever met," Hector said. He adds that while Rodrigo lived with the court rabbis, he studied history, science, agriculture, religion, languages, poetry, medicine, finance—and more. "I was fortunate to help him with his studies. I learned a lot just sitting near him. The rabbis had one of the best libraries in the world, and they let me use it. They treated me like a member of the family."

Hector is curious about everything on the island.

So, as we walk, I tell him about our crops: Cassava is our principal root crop, followed by sweet potato. We also cultivate maize, but we consider it inferior to cassava because the island's high humidity causes stored maize to become moldy. Other major crops are beans, peppers, squash and peanuts. We also grow calabashes, pineapple and cotton.

I add that children like to go into the pine forests to find wild fruits and vegetables, such as palm nuts, guava berries and guayiga roots.

Hector asks about fishing techniques, and I tell him men use nets, hooks and lines, and spears to catch fish. We sometimes store fish and turtles in weirs until we are ready to eat them.

One evening, sitting around a fire, he compliments me on my fluency in Spanish. "I taught Rodrigo Taíno, he taught me Spanish."

He asks if I can teach him to speak Taíno.

"Are you as good at languages as Rodrigo?"

He laughs and says, "No one is as good as Rodrigo—except perhaps you. But I do speak several languages—Spanish, Portuguese, French, Kikongo, Hebrew, Greek and Latin."

"Kikongo. What language is that?"

"That's the language of my native land, on the west coast of Africa. I learned it as a child before I was captured by the slave traders."

"When did the slave traders come?"

"I was just seven years old. They raided our village. Everyone ran, but I got caught. I don't know what happened to my mother and father and older brother. I hope they escaped. I just don't know. They put the ones they captured on three ships and sailed back to Europe. Two ships went to the slave market in Lisbon. My ship was taken to Spain, and those who survived the trip—many died and their bodies were thrown overboard—were taken to the slave market in Seville."

"How terrible!"

"I'm one of the few lucky ones. Rabbi Abraham bought me, freed me, and said I could work in his household as a paid employee. He said I was free to go, but since I had no place to go, I stayed with him more than 25 years until he died last year."

He tells me that he remembers that his family in Africa was Muslim. "Then I lived with a rabbi so long that I pretty much came to believe in Judaism. After the expulsion of the Jews, I was forced to become a Christian, although I was never formally baptized."

That evening, I pull out the Bible Queen Isabella gave me. "I can speak Spanish fairly well, but I can't read well. I'll trade you lessons in speaking Taíno if you'll teach me how to read better."

Hector looks at the Bible and tells me it's not written in Spanish—it's written in Latin. He says Latin was the language of the old Roman Empire, and that Spanish is derived from Latin. He says he can try to teach me to read Latin, but it won't be easy.

So, every day on the trail, I teach Hector how to speak Taíno. Every night, we pull out the Bible and Hector teaches me how to read Latin. He was right— it's not easy, but he says I'm doing remarkably well.

The night before we reach Caonabo's village, I realize Hector doesn't know Caonabo's story.

I tell Hector that Caonabo is the chief who led the attack and destroyed *Navidad.* "He's the biggest enemy of the Spaniards."

"I know of him. His name is known even in Spain," Hector answers.

I pull out my dagger. "Caonabo gave this to me."

Hector whistles as he examines the dagger.

I recount the story of the daggers, with emphasis on Anacaona's taking one from a Spaniard she killed defending her daughter.

"Must be quite a woman!" Hector says.

"She's the second most beautiful woman I've ever seen."

"Who's the first?"

"Her daughter, Mencia. My woman—now my wife."

"Tough, beautiful women, eh?"

"You will be doubly impressed."

After five days of walking, we reach Caonabo's village in the heart of the island.

My reunion with Caonabo and Anacaona is joyous. My reunion with Mencia is passionate.

I introduce Hector as 'my good friend', and he tells Caonabo and Anacaona, in Taínos, "It is my great honor to meet you both."

"Any friend of Guarocuya is a friend of ours!" Caonabo says, startled to hear Taíno words from the giant black man.

"You are a most handsome man, and you are welcome here," says Anacaona, smiling.

Hector tries but can't keep his eyes off Anacaona.

When I introduce Hector to Mencia, he says, in Taíno, "Guarocuya, you are a lucky man!"

"I am the lucky one," answers Mencia with a beautiful smile.

Again, Hector tries not to stare.

Chapter 27
Tribute to *Zemis*

Our arrival is well-timed. The village is preparing to hold its annual religious ceremony honoring its *zemis*—the major and minor gods of the Taínos.

"You'll learn a lot," I tell Hector.

Before the ceremonies, Anacaona takes Hector on a tour of the village.

"We decorate our pottery with *zemis*, which are representations of our gods," she tells Hector. "We also paint or carve *zemis* near caverns, rocks along the ocean, and other places where we think our gods live. Today we have gathered all our *zemis* for the ceremonies."

She tells us the ceremonies will be conducted by our priests and *bohuti* or shamans who paint themselves from head to toe with representations of different *zemis*. The ceremonies will take place in the large open space in front of Caonabo's large, square hut, or *bohio*, which today will serve as the village temple.

We are given seats of honor close to Caonabo. Anacaona sits next to him. Hector sits next to her, and Mencia and I sit next to Hector. Painted priests and shamans are stationed to our left and right. Hector agrees to let Anacaona paint his face with red and black markings. He is in good spirits.

"Our men will be communicating with our gods or *zemis*," Anacaona tells Hector. "You may join them, if you wish."

Caonabo starts the ceremonies by pounding a drum, soft and slowly at first. After he begins, we can hear other drums joining in from all corners of the village.

Villagers decorated with painted ornaments and *zemis* on their bodies form a procession and parade ceremoniously in front of Caonabo and his priests and guests.

Women carry baskets of fresh-baked cassava bread, which is intended to feed the village's *zemis*.

"Before communicating with the *zemis,* the men will have purified themselves by fasting, or by inserting a stick in their throat to cause vomiting," Anacaona whispers to Hector.

We watch as the men, holding personal or family *zemis*, parade before Caonabo. They use a forked tube to smoke *cohoba*—a snuff made from crushing the seeds of the piptadenia tree.

"The *cohoba* causes visions and dreams which enable each of the men to communicate with the *zemis,*" Anacaona tells Hector. "The men smoke it to learn the wishes of their *zemis*."

The village women, one by one, take bread to the priests who offer the breads to the *zemis*.

Some of the men, deep in visions, chant, sing, pray and bow to their *zemis*, to Caonabo's *zemis*, and to the *zemis* of dead chiefs.

"Some of the *zemis* here represent former chiefs, or belonged to former chiefs," Anacaona whispers in Hector's ear.

Priests offer prayers and ask for prosperity for the village—for plentiful rain, sunshine and healthy babies.

Anacaona begins singing, in a lovely soft voice. Mencia joins her. The village women add their voices. All villagers join in.

Anacaona nods to him, and Hector sings as well. I wonder about him: Born into a Muslim family, servant to a Jewish rabbi, forced to convert to Christianity. Now he's singing in one of our most sacred religious ceremonies.

The rhythm of the drums changes, the beats increasing in speed and sound. Everyone begins dancing.

Mencia takes me by the hand, and we dance.

Anacaona takes Hector's hand, and they dance.

Caonabo watches with a wide smile on his face. I see him smoke one of the forked pipes.

As we dance, the priests break off pieces of the cassava bread and pass them to the dancers, and to the old people watching from the sides.

"Don't eat all the bread," Anacaona tells Hector, her arms draped over his giant shoulders. "Save some of it. The fragments will protect you against accidents."

I watch Hector—once a slave, long a servant to a court rabbi—dancing in the wilderness with the second most beautiful woman in the world.

His face is decorated by paint and a huge smile.

Anacaona asks Hector if the Spanish have any festivals like this.

"We have a Psalm from the Bible that says: *Praise God with drums, and dance,*" he answers with a broad smile.

Hector and I both smoke from a forked pipe, as does Anacaona.

Mencia laughs at us.

I offer her the pipe, but she waves it away.

I try again, but she shakes her head and smiles at me.

I offer the pipe to her a third time. She refuses again.

"I have a secret," she whispers in my ear.

I stop dancing and stare at her. She is so beautiful. She is glowing.

She leans into to me and whispers again, "I must be careful. I don't want to give our baby bad dreams."

Our gods are good even if the times are bad.

Chapter 28
Mounds

The next morning, Mencia and I go to Caonabo and Anacaona to tell them that they soon will be grandparents. Anacaona acts surprised, but I guess she already knew Mencia is pregnant. Caonabo is unquestionably stunned—and pleased.

"I'm not quite 30 years old, and now I'm going to be a grandfather," he says. "Hard to believe—but what joyous news!"

We all hug, and I detect tears in the great chief's eyes.

After we eat and talk about possible names for the baby, Caonabo asks me to find Hector. "I want to show both of you something. I need help from both of you. It's important."

I'm puzzled, but ask no questions, and trot off to find Hector.

I find him still sleeping, and I shake him gently until he wakes with a moan.

"Caonabo wants to talk to you—to both of us."

He groans, and shakes my hand away.

"Let me sleep."

"He said it's important."

Hector groans again.

"What was in that thing we were smoking yesterday?" he asks. "I have a terrible headache. And my stomach is worse!"

I try, unsuccessfully to stifle a laugh.

"It's called *cohoba,* and it comes from crushing the seeds of a *piptadenia* tree. Everyone gets sick the first time they smoke it. Some people get sick every time, but not as badly as the first time."

"You should have warned me! Did I have terrible dreams!" he says with another groan.

"You'll survive. *Cohoba* is supposed to give you visions," I say and hand him a wooden bowl filled with fresh water. He takes a long drink, then pours the remainder over his head.

I can't help but laugh. He glares at me, and reminds me: "I'm twice your size. Don't make me angry!"

I laugh still again, and repeat that Caonabo wants to see us.

A groaning, disheveled Hector stands and grudgingly follows me to the chief's hut.

"Too much *cohoba?*" Anacaona asks, trying unsuccessfully to hide a smile.

"Ummm," he answers, but seeing her he stands straighter, runs his fingers through his hair and beard, and tries—not very successfully—to de-rumple his shirt and pants.

"Are you well enough to take a walk with me?" Caonabo asks, a kind smile on his face. "I know how *cohoba* can make you sick."

"A walk may clear my head."

At a leisurely pace to accommodate Hector, Caonabo leads us out of the village. We walk in a northerly direction toward the mountains. The sky is clear and blue, a soft breeze is blowing, and the temperature is mild.

"Feeling better?" Anacaona asks Hector.

"Fresh air is helping. I think I'll survive. But not sure."

Caonabo says nothing for the first thirty minutes of our walk until I ask, "Where are we going?"

"To a sad place."

I drop back and whisper to Anacaona, "Where's he taking us?"

"Burial grounds." She speaks softly.

After about another 40 minutes, the woods open to a beautiful glade with a gushing waterfall and gurgling stream nearby. Mountains tower over us.

Caonabo prays silently before he tells us: "This is where we buried the men who died fighting the Spanish."

We walk silently through the field of mounds. I watch Caonabo stopping to pray before each grave.

I add my silent prayers, as does Anacaona.

Hector stands at the edge of the glade, unmoving, head bowed. He seems to have shrunk. After a few moments, he rejoins us.

We gather near the waterfall, and Caonabo says, "Each man was buried as if he was a high chief, with his body flexed. *Zemis* are buried with them."

I silently count the mounds.

"Forty-seven," I say quietly. I'm relieved that the number isn't higher. I know Caonabo led some 2,000 men into battle.

"Most of my men fled at the first sight of the horses, and the sounds of the cannons," Caonabo says. "These graves are filled with the few men who stayed and fought."

I remember my recent meeting with Chief Guacanagari, and think of his son.

"Which one is Tuaymi's grave?" I ask.

Caonabo seems to flinch. He walks me to a grave near the middle of the mounds.

"He fought bravely. He didn't run when most of the others ran. He stayed at my side until a horse ran him down and a Spaniard ran a lance through him while he lay helpless on the ground."

"He was Guacanagari's only son."

"I know. I sent a messenger to Guacanagari to tell him of his son's death in hopes he would come and say prayers at his grave. He never answered."

"I talked to him," I say quietly.

"And he blames me for his son's death?" Caonabo ask.

I pause before answering, "Yes."

"He's right. I blame myself, too. I was foolish to think we could defeat the invaders as we did at *Navidad*."

"Do you think the outcome would have been different if your men hadn't fled?" Hector asks.

"I have thought about that for many hours, during many sleepless nights," Caonabo answers. "We will never know for sure, but it's probably good that so many fled—or we would have had to bury many more men here."

He's silent for a moment before adding: "One thing I learned from the battle is that no matter how many men we have we are no match for mounted soldiers with better weapons, cannon and war dogs. The invaders' horses simply terrified all of us."

We stare in silence at the burial mounds before Caonabo speaks again:

"I asked you to come here with me because I need your help. You know the invaders better than I do. I need you to tell me what we can do to defeat the invaders. If anything."

Chapter 29
Art of War

As we walk back to the village, Hector says he doubts he can help wage war on the Spaniards.

"I was never a soldier, just a slave who became a rabbi's servant."

"Can you tell me nothing?" Caonabo pleads.

"Rabbi Abravenel once hosted a Greek general who had studied Chinese military strategy. I remember being fascinated by what he said."

"Do you remember what he said?" Caonabo asks eagerly.

"I remember that he said there was a famous Chinese general—I can't remember his name—who wrote a book on the art of war. It was written hundreds of years ago."

"There was a lesson: 'If you know the enemy and know yourself, you need not fear the result of a hundred battles. If you know yourself but not the enemy, for every victory gained you will also suffer a defeat. If you know neither the enemy nor yourself, you will succumb in every battle'."

After pondering the lesson, Caonabo says: "We won the battle at *Navidad* but lost at *St. Tomas.* That means we know ourselves, but not the enemy. That makes sense. We had no idea what their war horses and cannon would mean in a battle. So, our men fled from the unknown."

"What else do you remember?" Anacaona asks Hector.

"There was another famous lesson: 'All warfare is based on deception. When you are able to attack, you must seem unable; when using forces, you must appear inactive; when you are near to the enemy, you must make the enemy believe you are far away; when you are far away, you must make the enemy believe you are near'."

"That makes sense," Caonabo says after pausing to digest Hector's words. "When we fought at *Navidad,* the Spaniards did not know we were coming, and were surprised. At *St. Tomas,* they knew we were coming, and met us with men and horses in armor, and with cannons and dogs."

"What else?" Anacaona asks.

Hector smiles, and says, "My favorite lesson was: 'Move swift as the wind and closely formed as the wood. Attack like fire and be still as the mountain'."

Caonabo smiles. "I like that. We can attack like fire and be still as the mountains. Do you remember anything else?"

Hector stops to think. He rubs his throbbing head with both hands.

"Oh yes! Spies are most important," Hector says. "The general said: 'What enables the good general to strike and conquer is foreknowledge. Knowledge of the enemy's dispositions can only be obtained from other men'."

Caonabo seems thunderstruck. He pauses, then looks at me—a look that makes me uneasy.

"I know you are the father of my grandchild soon to be born. But I need foreknowledge of what the Spaniards are going to do. Only you can do this because only you speak their language, and only you have friends inside their village. I need you to spy again."

I groan. I do not want to return to *Isabela.*

But I know I must. We Taínos can only win if we know what the Spaniards are planning.

Mencia will not be pleased when she learns I need to leave again, but she will understand. She knows we all must help her father fight the Spaniards.

At the outskirts of the village, Caonabo's sub-chief, Marieni, meets us.

"A messenger has arrived from Mayobanex. He has a message he will deliver only to you," Marieni says.

We hurry to Caonabo's hut where the messenger waits.

"Mayobanex told me to speak only to you, Chief Caonabo," the young messenger says. "No others are supposed to hear."

Caonabo waves all of us—Hector, Anacaona and me—out of the hut.

A few minutes later we see the messenger leave and begin his return trip home.

Caonabo waves us inside.

"What's happening?" Anacaona asks impatiently.

"The message was only this: 'Columbus has sailed away. He has left *Isabela.* Some Spaniards remain at *Isabela'*."

"What does that mean?" Anacaona asks.

"I wish I knew," Caonabo answers. "We must have more information. It is more important than ever that Guarocuya return to the Spanish village."

I don't want to leave my pregnant wife, and I don't want to live among the Spanish anymore.

But we need to know more, so Hector and I prepare to leave for *Isabela* early the next day.

Chapter 30
Caonabo's Value

At the last minute, Caonabo decides he wants to travel with Hector and me to *Isabela*—or at least as far as Mayobanex's village.

"I want to see for myself what's happening," he says.

"It's far too dangerous!" says Anacaona, shaking her head.

"I did it before!" Caonabo answers fiercely. "I went into *Isabela*—and even met Admiral Columbus—and none of the Spanish figured out who I was. I can do it again!"

"I agree with Anacaona," I say. "It's far too dangerous. You shouldn't have gone the first time. If the Spanish find out who you are—their worst enemy— you likely will be hanged! Or worse!"

"If they recognize you," adds Hector, "the only debate will be how to kill you—chop off your head, disembowel you and then cut you into quarters, hang you, or starve you to death and then hang you from their gibbet for all to see. Or burn you alive at the stake with green wood!"

Hector's rant leaves us speechless for a few moments.

"I can go again in disguise. I did it before," Caonabo says, but now his voice is less confident.

"Guacanagari and his people often visit *Isabela*. He would gladly identify you and enjoy watching you put to death," I say. "He would consider it revenge for Tuaymi's death."

"Everyone dies sometime," Caonabo answers. "If it's my time, it's my time."

I disagree: "You are special. The Spanish are terrified of you. They think they can enslave almost all the Taínos—they think we are not their equals. But they fear you. They shake at the mere mention of your name. They have sleepless nights because they fear you will attack at any minute. They are afraid to leave *Isabela* except in large military formations because they know you—Caonabo the warrior who destroyed *Navidad*—are out in the countryside, someplace—perhaps on the bluff signaling an attack!"

"It's true," Hector adds. "The name Caonabo is known in Spain as the warrior who burned the Spanish fortress at *Navidad* and killed all the Spaniards."

"Imagine how discouraged all the Taínos would be if the Spaniards caught you?" Anacaona adds. "You are our rallying point—our main hope that we can defeat the invaders."

"I'm not that important," Caonabo argues.

"Without their fear of you, the Spaniards would feel free to go anyplace, any time, and do anything they want," Hector answers.

"The Spanish really fear me that much?" Caonabo asks.

"Yes, they do," I answer.

"But your wife doesn't fear you," Anacaona says. "And I'm telling you that you're not going to visit *Isabela.*"

"Yes, my love," the fiercest and most-feared Taíno warrior says in mock meekness.

We all laugh, and sigh with relief.

"But I need to know, in detail, as soon as possible what the Spanish are doing," Caonabo says. "I can't rely on the short messages that runners bring me."

I regret that we Taínos have no a written language. The Spanish have so many advantages over us in the art of war—cannons, horses, dogs, iron, and a willingness—even an eagerness—to kill. Yet their greatest advantages may be the ability to transmit information in writing.

Caonabo promises he will go no farther than Mayobanex's village, and will not try to sneak into *Isabela.*

"We will ride Countess, the horse you gave us, so the trip shouldn't take long," Caonabo says.

Hector and I travel by foot fast and light on our trip to Mayobanex's village, and then to *Isabela.* Caonabo and Anacoana will follow on horseback in two weeks.

I picture Caonabo and Anacaona riding through the valleys, villages and mountains mounted on a horse. Their status among the Taínos can only soar.

We are slowed only by Hector's constant hunger. I can survive on small amounts of cassava bread, and berries and yams. But Hector, who must be twice my weight or more, seems to need four times the food I eat. He craves meat, so we have to stop at least once a day in villages and ask for food, especially fish.

The Taínos we meet, who gladly share their food, stare in wonder at the giant black man traveling with me.

When I say simply 'he is Caonabo's friend', we are welcomed—and fed—by all we meet.

Each day Taínos give us food that would feed their families for a week, but even so, Hector grumbles that he is always hungry.

He makes me laugh, and laughter is a good thing in these dark days.

Chapter 31
Spies Again

After three days of long, hard travel, we arrive at Mayobanex's village. To my disappointment, no one knows anything about events at *Isabela* even though the settlements are about five miles apart.

"I'm afraid to go there now that Admiral Columbus has gone," Mayobanex says. "The admiral was always friendly and assured me I was safe when I visited. The rest of the Spaniards are hostile, and they frighten me. Even Guacanagari avoids *Isabela*."

I tell him we've promised Caonabo that Hector and I will visit *Isabela* to spy on the Spaniards.

"Caonabo wanted to come with us to *Isabela* but we—mostly Anacaona—talked him out of it," Hector tells the chief.

"Thank the gods!" Mayobanex responds. "His wife is smarter than he is!"

We tell him that both Caonabo and Anacaona plan to come—on horseback—to Mayobanex's village within two weeks.

"Help us keep Caonabo from going to *Isabela!*" I plead to Mayobanex.

"I will! I don't think you two should go either. It's too dangerous!"

We nod in agreement, but we go anyway.

Early the next morning—when most of the Spaniards are still asleep—we enter *Isabela*. We're an odd pair—a small Taíno and a giant of a man from Africa. But we attract little notice at this early hour. We bring baskets of food, hoping gifts will please the Spaniards.

We go to Dr. Chanca's hut because he has always been kind to the Taínos.

He's eating a meager breakfast of hardtack and berries as we enter his sparse hut.

"Welcome!" he says with a smile. "It's Hector, right? You arrived on the *Nina?*"

"Yes, doctor, and you likely remember Guarocuya—Rodrigo's friend?"

"Of course! We have not seen many Indians around lately. I'm afraid they don't think it is safe here with the admiral gone. They're probably right, but it means we're not getting much in the way of fresh food from the Indians. Thank God the *Nina* brought supplies or we'd be starving."

"Where did Columbus go? And why?" Hector asks as he gives the baskets of food to the doctor.

"He just decided with no warning that he needed to go exploring—to find the mainland of India or China, or the Great Khan."

Chanca adds that Columbus took three caravels—the *Nina, San Juan* and *Cardera*—and sailed to the west.

"He ordered Rodrigo to go with him as translator," Chanca adds.

We are shocked and disappointed that Rodrigo is gone. We have so few friends.

"Who's in charge with the admiral gone?" Hector asks.

Chanca said Columbus appointed a council to rule in his absence. His brother, Diego, is chairman, and the other members are Fray Buil, Alonso Sanchez de Caravajal, Juan de Luxan and Captain Coronel.

"When will Columbus return?" Hector asks.

"He left on April 24 with enough provisions for about five months or so," Chanca answers. "He didn't leave us with many provisions, but told us that supply ships will arrive soon from Spain. I hope he's right."

He lowers his voice: "The men are starving and many are near mutiny. Most would like to sail home. The council has increased the guard on the ships—but who can be certain if the guards will remain loyal?"

The doctor suggests we visit with Columbus' brother, Diego. "He's a decent man, but I wonder if he's strong enough to handle this situation."

Diego is using the largest hut in the village—his brother's—built to house the island's viceroy.

A harried looking Diego waves us inside. "Happy to see you, Hector. I have a letter for you from your friend Rodrigo."

He hands the letter to Hector, who doesn't break the seal immediately.

Hector points to me and says, "You may remember Guarocuya. He, too, is a friend of Rodrigo."

"Oh yes!" Diego says. "Rodrigo told me Guarocuya has learned to speak a bit of Spanish, and could possibly serve as a translator. I've learned a bit of Indian talk, so maybe between the two of us we can work with the Indians."

Diego asks us where we are staying, and Hector answers that we have no plans.

"Stay with me then. My brother insisted that as chairman of the council I take the viceroy's hut in his absence. So, I have plenty of room. I'd enjoy some company. I'm not very popular right now. I won't let the men sail home."

What better place for spies than inside the home of the leader of the enemy?

Caonabo will be pleased. If we live to tell about it.

Hector and I walk to the edge of the village, check to see that no one is near, and break the seal on Rodrigo's letter.

It says only:

Beware Buil!

Chapter 32
Soulless

We return to the viceroy's hut, and that night, over a meager dinner that especially annoys Hector, Diego asks Hector, "What did Rodrigo say in his letter?"

"Only that he's gone with your brother looking for the Great Kahn, and that he expects they'll return in the fall."

"That's all?"

Hector pauses a moment before saying, "He warned us to be careful about Buil."

Diego points to the door and tells Hector, "Look outside and make sure no one is eavesdropping."

Hector goes to the door, walks around the hut and returns. He points two thumbs up. No one near.

Even so, Diego whispers.

"Fray Buil, a Benedictine monk. He is—by royal appointment—in charge of religious affairs for the colony. He is from Catalonia and is a friend of King Ferdinand. My brother and the king are not friends, and my brother and Buil are not friends."

He looks at Hector, who nods that he understands.

"Buil and my brother disagree on many things, including treatment of the Indians."

Hector nods for Diego to continue.

"Queen Isabela—my brother's chief supporter—wants our top priority to be the conversion of the Indians to Christianity. My brother also wants to save souls. Saving souls is critical in preparation for the Second Coming of Christ, which they believe is imminent."

Hector nods again.

"We have been here six months and not a single Indian has been baptized," Diego continues. "Buil, who is supposed to be in charge of converting the Indians, has no plans to baptize anyone."

"Why not?" Hector asks.

"Because Fray Buil believes Indians don't have souls."

"What?" Hector asks, astonished.

Diego stands up, walks to the entrance and looks outside the door to make sure again that no one is near. He returns, and resumes—without sitting down.

"Buil believes Indians are sub-human, that they are some kind of monkey," Diego says. "The Spanish have a rigid caste system. Non-humans are at the very bottom—maybe above horses, cows and pigs. Monkeys would be below the lowest human."

Diego, Hector and I sit in silence for several minutes before Hector asks Diego: "Why should we be concerned if Buil doesn't want to convert the natives to Christianity? They have their own gods."

"Everyone here is after gold, but we really haven't found much," Diego explains. "Not enough to satisfy King Ferdinand. Not enough to justify the expense of this voyage and maintaining the colony."

"But your brother says there are rivers of gold," Hector says.

"Maybe there are great gold mines on this island, but everyone is so terrified of Caonabo that we fear to travel anywhere without an army to protect us. That makes it difficult to find gold—if there is any. Buil and his followers are looking for other ways to gain quick fortunes. They want to convince my brother to go along with their scheme."

"Scheme?" Hector asks.

Diego looks at me before continuing, "If the Indians are sub-human and don't have souls, they could be shipped to Seville and sold on the slave market."

Hector looks shocked.

"Do you know, Diego, that I was once sold at the slave market in Seville?"

"No," he says, "I don't know your story."

Hector recounts his capture in Africa, his time as a slave, and his purchase by a court rabbi.

"That's how you know Rodrigo?"

Hector nods and adds: "After the rabbi died last year, I decided to follow Rodrigo here."

Diego points to me and asks, "What's this young Indian's story? Rodrigo told me he has learned how to speak a few words of Spanish and might be able to help as a translator."

"Can I tell him I traveled to Spain?" I ask Hector in Taíno.

Hector answers in Taíno, "No. Remember, the art of war requires deception."

I nod agreement and tell Diego that I met Rodrigo when he visited Guacanagari's village shortly after Columbus returned.

In half Spanish and half sign language, I tell Diego that Rodrigo asked for a guide to scout the area. "He taught me a few words of Spanish."

Diego nods that he accepts my story, adding: "Maybe I can help you learn more Spanish and you can teach me more Indian talk."

I wonder how he would have reacted if I'd I told him: "I'm not a monkey. I am your beloved queen's godson."

"If they are thinking about sending Taínos to the slave market, is Guarocuya safe? Should he leave?" Hector asks.

"Frankly, I fear for my life more from Spanish mutineers than from Caonabo," Diego answers. "I will announce that Guarocuya is our translator and under my personal protection."

Diego looks at Hector, grimaces and adds, "I may need to protect you as well. If they are looking to steal the ships, fill them with slaves and sail to Spain, they may want to grab you."

Hector scowls and says, "They won't take me alive."

Chapter 33
Shadow in Chief

Hector and I join Diego for a dinner of wormy biscuits, murky gravy and watered-down wine.

"Pretty sad for the president of the colony, isn't it?" Diego asks with a grim smile. "What I have, I gladly share with you."

I can't help but like Diego.

Hector suggests that he and I go to Mayobanex's village tomorrow and ask for bread and fish that we can bring to *Isabela.* I chuckle knowing that Hector is motivated by his ever-constant hunger that was far from satisfied by our poor meal tonight.

Diego tells us that since Hojeda cut off the innocent Indian's ears the Taínos have stopped bringing food to *Isabela.* The death rate among the Spaniards has increased as the amount of food has decreased.

"If the men were healthy, I'd have a mutiny on my hands," Diego says. "Bed-bound men make poor mutineers."

"Are the men manning the cannons loyal?" Hector asks, resuming our duties as spies.

"They are loyal mostly because they fear Caonabo," Diego answers. "We're pretty certain the cannons could drive off an attack. We also have horses and dogs ready to fight Caonabo, should he attack."

I see Hector look away so as to not meet my eyes. We already have learned much. Curse the dogs and horses and cannons. And Pope Borgia.

We eat in silence for several minutes before Diego says, "Maybe you're wondering why I'm here, living in the wilderness among people who don't respect or like me. Some even hate me. The truth is I have no dreams of my own. So, I've followed my brother, who has dreams enough for everyone. My brother left me in charge for one reason only—he knows he can trust me."

Diego looks at Hector, who simply nods that he'd like to hear more of the story.

"Our father was a poor weaver in Genoa. What little education we received was thanks only to the Cappucciati monks who rented a small house to my father near the gate of Saint Andrea. Genoa once owned the monopoly to trade in the Black Sea, but after the Sultan of Turkey captured Constantinople in 1453—when Christopher was just two years old—Genoa was barred from the Black Sea by the Turks. That caused great hardship in Genoa, and our father lost everything, and he even had to spend time in a debtor's prison."

I'm fascinated by Columbus' childhood story.

"Christopher has been hugely ambitious for as long as I've known him. He refused to follow my father as a weaver, and looked to the sea for salvation. He took all kinds of menial jobs so he could learn sailing and trading. He taught himself everything he could about seamanship, geography and mapmaking. Our other brother, Bartholomew—the middle son—learned mapmaking as well, and he and Christopher spent many years in Lisbon studying the seas, making maps, and dreaming together of sailing west to reach the Spice Islands."

"Where's Bartholomew?" Hector asks.

Diego says that after the King of Portugal refused to finance their voyages, Bartholomew went to England to seek funding from King Henry VII while Christopher sought funding from Queen Isabela.

He added that Columbus hoped Bartholomew would reach Cadiz in time to sail on the Second Voyage, but the fleet had to sail before he arrived.

"So, Christopher is stuck with me, the ineffectual brother without ambition, as his second in command."

"Do you expect Bartholomew to come here?" Hector asks.

"I look to the sea every day, hoping to see sails. Bartholomew is much more practical than Christopher and has much more of a commanding presence than I will ever have."

Hector looks at Diego in puzzlement.

"Christopher has his dreams of greatness and thinks he is guided by God. Bartholomew could be a general who leads armies into battle," Diego explains. "Me, I have no dreams of my own. I just follow my brother like a shadow with no substance of my own."

Chapter 34
Mayobanex's Offer

We spend several more days spying at *Isabela*.

We learn that the Spanish command nearly 30 cannon, mounted on the two remaining ships. They are aimed strategically to repel an attack by Caonabo, and the Spaniards have many rounds of cannon balls. Captain Pedro Fernandez Coronel, one of the five appointed by Columbus to the ruling council, is in command of the cannons. He would like to kill Indians.

Alonso Sanchez de Carvajal—also a member of the ruling council—is in charge of the horses and dogs. He casually assures Hector that there are enough healthy men who can ride the horses into battle. "Our horses will trample the damned Indians. Our dogs will devour their bodies!"

Diego says he is confident in the loyalty of Carvajal and Fernandez Coronel, but is uncertain about the loyalties of Juan de Luxan, the fifth council member. "When he does talk to me, he is guarded. I know he doesn't like foreigners—meaning my brother and me."

How about Buil? Hector asks.

"One thing I'm certain of is that Fray Buil is our enemy. He also hates Indians," Diego says. "Luxan normally sides with Buil. But as long as Captain Carvajal and Fernandez Coronel remain loyal, we have three votes and control of the council."

We try to approach Buil, just to talk, but he sees us at his door, and snarls, "I don't want a cursed son of Cham and a dirty Indian in my hut! Keep your filthy bodies out!"

"That's all we need to know," Hector says.

"Who is Cham?" I ask.

"It's a false claim from the Bible that says the descendants of Cham—or his son Canaan—are cursed with darkness of the skin and obliged to serve whites," Hector says quietly but angrily. "It's an excuse for slavery that's been used for hundreds of years!"

***

We tell Diego we will be leaving *Isabela* to travel to Mayobanex's village in hopes of obtaining food for *Isabela.*

"We need help desperately," Diego says.

"Why is your brother's friend, Chief Guacanagari, not supplying you with food?" Hector asks.

"That's a sad story," Diego says. "Guacanagari asked my brother if his dead son could be baptized so he could go to Heaven when the Second Coming occurs."

I am stunned, but say nothing about knowing Guacanagari's son Tuaymi or his death during the recent battle with the Spanish.

"Guacanagari, my brother and your friend Rodrigo—acting as translator—went to Fray Buil, who is in charge of converting the Indians to Christianity. They asked if he could save Guacanagari's son's soul—baptize him even after he died. Guacanagari said he also wished to be baptized. Buil just laughed and told them: 'Indians—alive or dead—don't have souls that can be saved. They are not human'."

Hector and I look at Diego in shock.

"Guacanagari fled *Isabela* in tears, and we haven't seen him or any of his people—or their food—since," Diego adds. "My brother was very upset. That's when he decided to take the three ships and go look for the mainland of India. He'd much rather be an explorer than a governor."

Hector and I also are glad to flee *Isabela.* Mayobanex greets us warmly when we enter into his village late the next day. He tells us Caonabo and Anacaona have yet to arrive.

We share with him all that we have learned in *Isabela.*

When we ask for food for the Spaniards, Mayobanex responds, "We will not help them. They killed our men who fought with Caonabo—that was expected in battle. But then they cut off the ears of an innocent man, and left him to die. And then they captured three innocent men and took them to *Isabela* to be executed. They were only freed because we begged Admiral Columbus for their lives."

"We know," Hector responds.

"Do you know that right now Spaniards are roaming the island raping women, stealing gold and food and killing any Taíno who resists?" Mayobanex asks.

"How can that be?" I ask. "Columbus sailed away with many of his men, and the rest of the men at *Isabela* are too sick to do anything."

"It's not the men at *Isabela.* It's the Spaniards Columbus left behind at Fort Tomas," Mayobanex answers. "More than 200 Spaniards are there, raping and pillaging. If Caonabo calls for another army, he'll have many volunteers—including me!"

"I wonder if Diego knows what's happening at Fort St. Tomas?" Hector asks.

"Perhaps Diego would order them to stop in exchange for food," I suggest.

Mayobanex guides us to a bluff overlooking the Spanish village.

"I'll agree to deliver fish, bread and vegetables to the Spanish," Mayobanex tells us, "but only if Diego stops what's going on at the Spanish fort in the mountains."

We wait several days to no avail for Caonabo and Anacaona to arrive—and for Hector to fill his huge empty belly with fresh fish and vegetables—before we reluctantly return to *Isabela* to present Mayobanex's offer to Diego.

Diego is not surprised to hear about the Spanish rampages at Fort St. Tomas.

"They've sent messengers asking for food, and we had none to send," he says. "They have only trinkets to buy food from the Indians. I know they have no respect for the Indians. They are inviting another *Navidad* massacre."

"Can you agree to Mayobanex's offer?" Hector asks.

"I'll have to ask the council," Diego answers. "Do you think he'd be willing to provide food for both *Isabela* and Fort Tomas?"

"We can ask," answers Hector. "The Taínos are furious that their women are being raped and their men killed and maimed. I warn you that Caonabo has only to ask, and he will have thousands—perhaps tens of thousands—of men ready to go to war."

Chapter 35
It's a Deal, for Now

At mid-morning the next day, Diego Colon calls the ruling council to order, and asks Hector to explain Mayobanex's offer. I sit at Hector's side in case I can help answer questions.

Hector says the offer is very simple: Mayobanex is willing to resume bringing food—fish, fruits and vegetables—if the Spanish at Fort St. Tomas stop raping and pillaging.

At Diego's request, Dr. Chanca reminds the council that many of the Spaniards are sick and all are hungry. "We bury men nearly every day," the doctor adds. "If you want the sick to live, we need more and better food."

Chanca adds that most of the healthy Spaniards—and most of the supplies aboard the *Nina*—sailed with Admiral Columbus in his quest to find the mainland of India.

Diego repeats that the Spaniards in charge at Fort St. Tomas—Mosen Pedro Margarit and Alonso de Hojeda—have sent requests to *Isabela* for food.

"Their men are starving, too," Diego adds. "We have no food to send them. If we agree to his proposal, we can send some of Mayobanex's food to St. Tomas."

Diego asks for the council members' thoughts.

"We can't trust Indians," Fray Buil says. "I'm opposed. We shouldn't negotiate. We should take our horses and cannon to Mayobanex's village and take everything we want. I can't believe we are even considering negotiating with these animals."

"I agree with Fray Buil—except I'm very hungry," says council member Juan de Luxan. "I don't see what alternative we have. I don't think we have enough healthy men to march on Mayobanex's village."

Buil glares at Luxan, who shrugs.

"When can we expect to get ships with supplies from Spain?" council member Alonso Sanchez de Carvajal asks.

Diego says Antonio de Torres sailed 12 of our ships home in February, and planned to return as soon as possible with fresh supplies and men.

"We simply have no idea when he will return," Diego adds. "Just remember that the seas—and the politics at court—are dangerous at times. We don't even know if they reached Spain safely."

Fernandez Coronel, the fifth council member, says, "I don't think we have much choice. We need to somehow hold out until Torres returns. Once we get resupplied, we can reconsider our arrangement with the Indians, but until then we'd better get along with Mayobanex."

"It's that or starve," Luxan adds.

"Unfortunate but true," says Coronel.

"I agree," adds Carvajal.

"Then the vote is 4-1," Diego says. "I will send Margarit a letter reminding him that Admiral Columbus assigned him command at Fort St. Tomas and ordered him in writing to do the Indians no harm."

Fray Buil stands up, snorts in derision and walks out of the meeting.

"That's part of our problem," Diego mutters. "Buil is in charge of making the Indians Christians. Instead, he is making them into our enemies."

The next day, Diego sends Margarit a formal letter—speaking as president of the council—commanding him to stop mistreating the Indians in exchange for food.

After we watch Diego's messenger leave *Isabela,* Hector and I go to Mayobanex village, and find—to our pleasure—that Caonabo and Anacaona have arrived.

We recount to the three of them the details of the Spanish council meeting, and many other details from our spy mission.

"So maybe we will have peace," Mayobanex says. "Maybe the Spanish have learned that they need us as friends."

Anacaona shakes her head and says, "Didn't you hear them say that they will live by this agreement only until they receive supplies from Spain?"

"We need to somehow stop the stealing and raping," Caonabo says wearily. "I hate burying my men. No matter how big an army I raise, I'm not sure we can defeat armored men, cannon, and war horses and dogs."

"Maybe the Spanish have learned that they need us as friends if they want to survive," Mayobanex repeats.

"What do you think?" Caonabo asks Hector and me.

"The Spanish don't treat people who aren't full-blooded Christian Spaniards with respect," Hector responds. "I don't think you can trust them."

Caonabo looks at me.

"You can't trust them," I say.

"Why not?" asks Mayobanex.

"They don't consider us equals. Many of the Spaniards think we are monkeys."

"What are monkeys?" Mayobanex ask.

"Animals that live in jungles," Hector answers. "Creatures without souls—creatures of less stature even than black slaves from Africa."

We spend six pleasant days at Mayobanex's village, visiting with Caonabo and Anacaona, and talking about Mencia's pregnancy and wondering about the child who is about to join us. At night, I dream about a wonderful world for my child, and wake to the reality that the Spaniards have brought only nightmares.

Hector, to the amusement of the Taínos, spends most of his time eating. "I'm just hungry," he says to their laughter.

On the sixth day, Caonabo and I walk to a high bluff overlooking the ocean so he can view *Isabela* from a safe distance.

To our shock, we see three ships on the horizon, heading toward the Spanish village.

"Could that be Columbus returning?" Caonabo asks.

"Maybe," I say, squinting in hopes of seeing better. "But I don't recognize the *Nina,* the ship I know best."

Caonabo turns to me, puts an arm on my shoulder, and says, "I need you to spy once more."

I feel a sense of gloom.

Chapter 36
The Third Brother

Diego Colon is smiling broadly when Hector and I find him in the viceroy's hut.

"Whose ships are those?" Hector asks, pointing to newly arrived carvels.

"Queen Isabela and King Ferdinand gave them to my brother, Bartholomew," Diego says jubilantly.

"Your brother?" Hector asks.

"Yes. He just arrived with them—and they are full of food, medicine and healthy men! The king and queen also sent a letter approving of everything the admiral has accomplished!"

Just then, the door to the hut swings open, and a tall, swaggering, heavily bearded stranger enters.

"This is my brother, Bartholomew," Diego tells us deferentially. "He met with the king and queen when their court was at Valladolid. They designated him *caballero,* so you should address him as Don Bartholomew."

Hector bows, and says, "Don Bartholomew."

I mimic Hector and bow, but say nothing.

Brusquely, Bartholomew asks Diego, "And who are these two—this big black man, and this little Indian?"

"They are helping us get food from the neighboring Indian village," Diego answers timidly.

Almost rudely, Bartholomew demands of Hector: "Who's your master?"

"I am a free man, your grace, and I have papers to prove it," Hector answers calmly, and a bit defiantly. "One of the court's rabbis, Isaac Abravenel—a great friend of the Queen—bought me at the Seville slave market many years ago and freed me. I am a long-time friend of Rodrigo de Triana."

"You have ties to a rabbi and to Rodrigo the Jew? Are you a Jew?"

"At the queen's request, Isaac Abravenel and all who worked for him, including me, renounced Judaism so we could remain in Spain," Hector replies.

"Then are you a false Jew fleeing from the Inquisition?" Bartholomew asks in an accusatory tone.

"No, Don Bartholomew."

"Are you a Templar, carrying secret messages, hoping to thwart our most holy pope?"

Hector blinks and hesitates for a second before saying, "No, Don Barthlomew."

I wonder how many lies Hector just told, then remember that deception is a part of war. We are at war.

Bartholomew turns to me, and asks Diego, "And who is this Indian? He could be a spy!"

"He's a friend," Diego answers meekly. "We've had trouble with the Indians—especially with a warlike chief named Caonabo—and the Indians have stopped supplying us with food. This young Indian has learned a little bit of Spanish, and has helped us reach an agreement with the nearest chief so we can be supplied with food."

"You don't need to go begging to the Indians anymore!" Bartholomew says belligerently, shaking his head at his younger brother. "My ships are full of food and medicine. Looks like I arrived just in time!"

"Everyone here is delighted at your timely arrival. Our brother left me in charge in his absence, but I am happy to turn the presidency over to you," Diego says.

The older brother nods his head, and says, "From everything I have heard, you are facing a mutiny. Now that I'm here there will be no further allowances for mutineers. I'll whip the first man I hear talking mutiny, cut off the ears of the second, and hang the third. That will put an end to any mutiny."

"Yes, your arrival is most timely," Diego says meekly.

"And we won't be lenient with the Indians either. Fray Buil told me the council—over his objection—agreed to the Indians' demands. He says we need to be tougher on the Indians."

Diego shrugs, and says: "We've been starving. Dr. Chanca told the council that the sick would die if we didn't get more food. The Indians said they'd give us food if the Spaniards at Fort St. Tomas would stop stealing and raping."

Bartholomew motions impatiently for his younger brother to continue.

"The council sent Mosen Pedro Margarit an order to stop mistreating the Indians, reminding him that both the admiral and Queen Isabela want the Indians treated kindly and baptized."

Bartholomew softens, and says, "Quite right. Margarit must follow our brother's orders, and the wishes of Queen Isabela. When I met with the queen and king, Isabela made me swear that I would treat the Indians well, and that we are all to remember that conversion of the natives is our top priority."

"That hasn't gone well," Diego says. "Fray Buil is in charge of baptizing the natives, and so far, he hasn't baptized a single soul. Buil thinks the Indians are some sort of monkey."

"He may be right," Bartholomew answers, "but if Queen Isabela wants souls saved—we will save souls, even monkey souls."

He looks at me, and says, "This little fellow does look like some kind of monkey."

I want to scream, and tell him that Queen Isabela is my godmother, and King Ferdinand is my godfather. That the queen gave me a ring, and a Bible. And that her children are friends who gave me gifts.

But Hector, sensing my anger, tugs my elbow gently, shakes his head almost imperceptibly, and I say nothing.

"We have yet to hear from Margarit at Fort Saint Tomas," Diego tells his brother. "We need him to follow our orders—the queen's commands, our brother's orders, and the council's ruling."

"He will, or we'll hang him," Bartholomew says. "Sometimes the best thing a new leader can do is to make an example of a troublemaker."

"Margarit is a friend of the king," Diego says.

Bartholomew smiles, and says, "We need to show that here our brother is the viceroy. No one can challenge his authority. A hanging can prove that point—especially if we hang a friend of the king."

Chapter 37
Mutiny

Mosen Pedro Margarit has no intention of being hanged.

He arrives in *Isabela* two days later—in full armor, riding a fierce war horse, and accompanied by more than 60 armed men.

Some of the men ride horses, others restrain snarling war dogs. Each of Margarit's men is armed with either a crossbow, a cuirass, a harquebus or an iron-tipped spear.

"Mutiny. Big time," Hector whispers to me.

While his small army circles around him, Margarit rides his giant steed to the viceroy's hut and demands to see Diego Colon.

Diego exits the hut accompanied by Bartholomew.

"This is my brother, Bartholomew, who has just arrived here after meeting with Queen Isabela and King Ferdinand," Diego says.

"What is the meaning of this?" Bartholomew demands, taking charge.

Margarit throws down to the ground a document. "This is what I think of the council's order."

He spears the document, lifts it to his hands, and tears it into pieces.

"Do you come to challenge the authority of the viceroy, whose authority comes from Queen Isabela and King Ferdinand?" Bartholomew demands angrily.

"By this order, the council has defamed my reputation as a *caballero!*" Margarit shouts. "Admiral Columbus appointed me to my position—not this weak-kneed council. The admiral's written orders conferred on me—and I quote—'the same power that I hold from Their Highnesses of Viceroy and Captain General of these Indies'. The council has no authority over me or my men!"

I look around, and note that most of the men of are smiling. The admiral's brothers have few, if any, supporters.

Except for Dr. Chanca, who says, "I urged Diego Colon and the rest of the council to send you the letter asking that you stop mistreating the Indians. Most of the men here are sick, and we need food to keep them from dying. The Indians have been withholding help because they are angry at their treatment by you and your men. They said they would bring us food and water if you and your men stop raping and pillaging."

"Doctor, you are a brave man, and I will spare your life because you have saved many lives," Margarit answers. "But my honor has been challenged, and I will not stand for it! If the sick need food, my men will go into the Indian villages and get you whatever you need. We should not be down on our knees begging the Indians for help—not when we can just take whatever we want! Remember that the pope has given this land to us!"

Bartholomew steps a foot forward, and says: "I have brought food and medicine on my three ships. We have plenty now. We need not negotiate with the Indians any further."

Margarit laughs as Fray Buil walks to his side.

"You may want to keep up your begging," Buil cackles.

"What are you saying?" Bartholomew demands.

"Captain Margarit and I have been meeting," Buil says, a great smirk on his face. "We've decided to return to Spain, where we tell everyone at court that this whole venture is a fraud. There is no gold, no spices, no royal princes, and no souls to save. We will unmask your lying, pretentious brother for the great fraud he is!"

"How do you propose to return to Spain?" Bartholomew asks.

"On those three ships," Margarit answers, pointing at the caravels Bartholomew just arrived in.

"Those are my ships!" Bartholomew. "Not only will you be committing mutiny, you will be pirates and thieves!"

"The ships actually belong to the sovereigns," Margarit says with a laugh. "We are not taking the ships from you—we are returning them to King Ferdinand and Queen Isabela."

"That's outright theft! Those are my ships, and my brothers' supplies. They were provided by the king and queen for their viceroy and their subjects!"

Buil's smile broadens, and he says, "Captain Margarit and I are both great friends of King Ferdinand. We know well that he has little, if any, regard for your brother. We are quite confident that once we tell Ferdinand the truth behind this fraudulent venture, he will protect us—even help us put an end to this bogus scheme concocted by a lying foreigner."

"You both will hang—as will any who participate in this mutiny!" Bartholomew shouts.

"I can imagine the day when your brother—and the two of you—are shipped home in chains," Buil says.

Margarit turns his horse around and announces, "Anyone who wants to join us and return to Spain may do so. Anyone who opposes us will be put to death."

A great hurrah come from the men.

"But there will not be room for all," Margarit says. "The sick will have to remain. We will leave the medicine and some food here with Dr. Chanca."

Hector and I slip out of *Isabela,* and rush to Mayobanex's village to tell Caonabo about the mutiny.

"Margarit and Buil are stealing the ships?" Caonabo asks in astonishment.

"I doubt anyone can stop them," Hector answers.

"At least, there will be fewer Spaniards here to rape our women and steal our food," Anacaona says.

Three days later, five of us—Caonabo, Anacaona, Mayobanex, Hector and I—climb to a high point on the bluff to observe *Isabela*, and we watch the three ships sailing away.

"What will happen now?" Caonabo asks Hector as the ships disappear into the offing.

He shrugs.

"They could be convicted of mutiny and hanged, or they could cause Admiral Columbus terrible problems. I expect King Ferdinand will protect them because he has never liked Admiral Columbus."

"What perplexes me the most about the Spaniards," says Anacaona, "is not their terrible greed, or even their violence, but rather their coldness, and their hardness, and their lack of love, even for each other."

Chapter 38
The Other Cheek

We talk for long hours, sitting on the bluff overlooking *Isabela* and the ocean, about what we should do next.

Caonabo, the warrior the Spaniards most fear, is hesitant to do battle again, even knowing that thousands of Taínos are ready to go to war should he decide to raise an army.

"With the men at *Navidad,*" he says, "it was somewhat easy. We ambushed many of the Spaniards when they wandered the island. There were just ten or so Spaniards when we raided *Navidad,* and we simply out-numbered them. They didn't have cannon, or dogs—or most importantly, horses. We can't fight men in armor on horseback, backed by cannons."

We debate whether we can attack *Isabela* now that most of the remaining Spaniards are ill and ill-nourished.

"Even though Buil and Margarit and many of the Spaniards have left, they did not take any of the war horses or dogs. And the Spaniards still have their cannons."

"How about trying again to be their friends?" Mayobanex asks timidly. "Perhaps the worst of the worst Spaniards sailed away with Fray Buil and Margarit."

Anacaona shakes her head in disagreement, but adds, "If my husband doesn't want to raise another army, we can try to be their friends. If that doesn't work, we will know for certain that battle is our only alternative."

Caonabo only nods slowly in sad agreement. "War must be our last resort."

Mayobanex looks at me and asks my opinion.

"I wonder if we shouldn't let them starve to death," I answer.

After a long silence, Hector tells us: "I remember that in the Christian Bible, their Savior, Jesus Christ, preaches:

Love your enemies, do good to those who hate you, bless those who curse you, pray for those who abuse you. To one who strikes you on the cheek, offer the other cheek also. Give to everyone who begs from you, and from one who takes away your goods do not demand them back. As you wish that others would treat you, do so to them."

Anacaona looks long at Hector, then laughs bitterly. "So, you think we should live by their Bible, when they do not?"

Hector only shrugs, and says, "In truth, I don't know what to think."

But after hours more of discussion, we decide to 'turn the other cheek'.

Perhaps their powerful One God will appreciate our kindness.

So, the Taínos begin to regularly deliver to our enemies at *Isabela* cassava bread, sweet potatoes, corn, peppers, peanuts, fish of all kinds, clams, conches, turtles, papayas, pineapples, plums, pears and other foods.

Dr. Chanca often says thanks, and 'God Bless you', and tells us we are saving lives.

Diego Colon also thanks us, but his brother, Bartholomew, only asks—demands—that we bring more. And he curses the Spaniards who are too ill or too haughty to till the soil, or hunt, or even fish. Or raid the Taíno villages.

Alfonso de Ojeda, who took over command of Fort St. Thomas after Margarit left for Spain, learns what we're doing in *Isabela,* and asks us for food, too, and we bring food to him and his men, too. All in the name of peace.

And for a time, the Spaniards stop stealing our possessions and raping our women.

"Maybe there is something good about the Spaniard's Bible," Mayobanex says after several months of relative calm.

"Are there other teachings from the Bible we should know?" Caonabo asks Hector.

Hector smiles grimly, and answers: "In the Jewish Bible. The Book of Leviticus, it is said:

Fracture for fracture, eye for eye, tooth for tooth. The one who has inflicted the injury must suffer the same injury."

"So that's an option—even by Christian standards?" Anacaona asks without expecting an answer. She pulls out her dagger and says, "Eye for eye."

I still think we should let the Spaniards starve.

Chapter 39
Return

In late September—while Hector and I are bringing cassava bread, fruits and vegetables to *Isabela*—we hear joyful shouts of 'sails on the horizon!'

Even the sick rise from their beds and rush to the water's edge to witness the arrival of ships—great events that break days of monotony, boredom and despair.

As sails rise out of the offing, the men shade their eyes against the afternoon sun in hopes of identifying the ships.

"I see three ships," one Spaniard calls out.

"Caravels," says another.

"Spanish insignias," says a third.

"Perhaps Buil and Margarit had to turn back?" speculates another.

"I think one is the *Nina,*" I say quietly to Hector. I hope so because it would mean the return of our friend Rodrigo.

A sailor who'd climbed up the rigging of the anchored flagship *Margarita* for a better view calls out, "It's Columbus' fleet returning—the *Nina, San Juan* and the *Cardera.*"

A groan rolls through the men on the beach.

"Why are they groaning?" I ask Hector.

"Ships from Spain will come with fresh supplies—food, medicine and rum. Instead, these three ships will return with men who have run out of food. More mouths to feed."

Hector told me earlier that most of the men don't like Columbus, and think they'd have a better chance of going home if he never returned. If Columbus is on Hispaniola—with his royal authority—it's much more dangerous to plot mutiny.

Two men overjoyed at the admiral's return are his brothers, Bartholomew and Diego, who row out in a small boat to greet the admiral.

We watch from the beach as the brothers climb aboard the *Nina,* but there is no sign of the admiral. The sailors we see have long, unkempt beards.

The boat that took the brothers to the *Nina* is rowed back to the beach, and Dr. Chanca is located and taken hurriedly to the *Nina.*

A few men climb down ropes from the ships' decks and swim and wade to shore—including, to our delight, Rodrigo.

Hector and I wave vigorously to attract his attention.

After he reaches shore, Rodrigo shakes water off his body and gestures for us to follow him. We move away from the crowd so we can't be overheard.

"We're glad you're back safely!" Hector says, reaching to hug his lifelong friend.

Rodrigo holds up his hands to stop our greetings, and whispers, "Admiral Columbus may be dying."

We stare at him, waiting for details.

"We ran out of supplies two weeks ago, the weather was often terrible, the *Nina* ran aground and was almost lost," Rodrigo says. "The natives were sometimes hostile and sometimes friendly. Columbus did a masterful job of sailing—but he didn't sleep for days on end."

Rodrigo tells us the small fleet explored the entire south coast of Cuba—Columbus renamed it Juana in honor of Queen Isabela's oldest daughter—and circumnavigated the island of Jamaica.

"I don't think we were anywhere near India, China or Japan," he adds. "We didn't bring back any gold or pearls. Don't tell anyone anything."

"Why should we keep that secret?" Hector asks.

"Columbus thinks differently," Rodrigo answers. "All indications are that Cuba is just another large island. That's what all the natives told us. That's what the currents indicated. But Columbus claims Cuba is a peninsula of Asia. He believes that if we could have sailed just a bit farther, we would have found the Great Khan."

"Is he delusional?" Hector asks.

"He wants to report back to court that he's reached India," Rodrigo says, shaking his head. "He made every man on the three ships sign a notarized document claiming we'd reached a peninsula of Asia. He plans on sending the document to court as proof that he's reached India."

"Did you sign it?" Hector asks.

"Everyone—myself included—signed it," he says. "We were out of food and fresh water. The weather was terrible with severe thunderstorms. Many of us were sick, and all of us were frightened. We feared Columbus wouldn't turn back for *Isabela* unless we signed. The men figured they had three choices— die, mutiny or sign the document and return to *Isabela*."

"What's wrong with Columbus?" I ask.

"He has a high fever, he goes in and out of a coma, and he's often delirious. He's gone blind. He has dysentery and gout. Part of it may be just physical exhaustion from not sleeping, and lack of food and water. I had no medicine to help him."

We watch as a litter is lowered from the *Nina's* deck into a small boat, and the comatose admiral is rowed ashore, and then carried into the viceroy's hut, his anxious brothers and Dr. Chanca trailing his litter.

I see the men of *Isabela* watching, no pity on their faces.

Chapter 40
4,000 a Year

Days, weeks and months go by with little trouble with the Spaniards.

Mayobanex's village continues to provide food to *Isabela*. We hear that Columbus is slowly recovering his health, and is no longer blind. His brothers are overseeing slow but somewhat steady construction of the Spanish settlement.

We are lulled into a false sense of security, and I return to Caonabo's village to live with Mencia and our new son.

Mencia and I are playing joyfully in the afternoon sun with our baby son when Rodrigo and Hector arrive unexpectedly.

Carrying terrifying news.

"Tell everyone to run into the mountains and hide!" Rodrigo says to Caonabo. He urges Caonabo to send warnings to every village, and to tell all Taínos to stay hidden until the danger is past.

"Be prepared to stay in hiding for a long time!" Hector adds.

"What is happening?" an incredulous Caonabo asks as we gather in his hut.

Hector tells us Columbus has decided to capture Taínos and ship them to Spain to be sold at the slave market in Seville.

As I hear his words, I remember Hector's history at the same slave market.

"Slaves?" Anacaona asks in astonished bewilderment.

"Slavery has been legal in Spain and Portugal since 1452 when Pope Nicholas V approved the right to enslave anyone who is not a practicing Christian," Hector, the expert on slavery, tells us. "His papal bull known as *Dum Diversas* allows Portugal and Spain to buy slaves from Africa—where the people had never heard of Christianity—and allows pagans to be consigned to 'perpetual servitude'."

"As far as I know," Rodrigo adds, "no Taínos have been baptized since the Spanish arrived. That means the Christians consider all of you to be pagans—and eligible to be sold into slavery."

I remember being baptized at court in Barcelona many months ago. The queen shed tears, hugged me and made me her godson. I went to mass with her many times, learned Christian prayers, and knelt before the bloodied Savior on the crucifix. But I still trust my Taíno gods, and say prayers to them only.

"How can Queen Isabela permit this?" I ask.

"They are going to lie to her," Rodrigo says. "Columbus plans to capture a thousand to 1,500 Taínos in the next few weeks. He will pick the best 500 to send to the slave market in Seville. He will tell Queen Isabela they are pagans and cannibals."

Hector adds grimly: "The admiral has issued orders to capture both men and women—and he thinks naked young women will attract premium prices."

Anacaona moans.

"How do you know this?" a shocked Caonabo asks.

"Everyone in *Isabela* knows it," Hector answers. "Columbus announced the news to all the Spaniards in an effort to quell another mutiny. Instead of gold, he said everyone can make a fortune capturing and selling slaves."

Rodrigo tells us that Columbus estimates there are between 500,000 and one million Taínos on the island—and more on neighboring islands such as Cuba, Jamaica and Puerto Rico.

"That's a gold mine—a gold mine of slaves," Rodrigo adds.

We look at him in disbelief.

"Their plan is to sell four thousand Taínos a year! They believe they can maintain the slave market at that rate for many years," Hector adds.

We are stunned. Four thousand a year.

The last time I saw Columbus he was unconscious, on the verge of death and being carried into his hut at *Isabela*. The Spanish were staving off starvation by accepting charity from the Taínos. They seemed likely to mutiny and kill the brothers from Genoa.

"I have done nothing to organize a new army," says Caonabo. "I thought the island would be at peace, at least while the Spanish depend on us for food."

"What's changed?" asks Anacaona.

Rodrigo answers that the admiral's health improved, and he regained his ability to make bold promises. Second, he made his brother Bartholomew, second in command, and he has become a very powerful voice for action—Bartholomew has hanged several Spaniards for plotting mutiny. Third, four caravels under the command of Antonio de Torres, arrived at *Isabela* from Spain, bringing much-needed supplies—which made help from the Taínos less critical.

"Also, Torres brought warnings from court that Columbus had better bring back gold—or something of equal value—to Spain soon. Or face the wrath of King Ferdinand," Rodrigo says.

"Columbus is desperate," Hector adds. "Slaves will replace gold."

We know that Columbus hasn't made good on his promises of finding rivers of gold, valuable spices, the Great Khan, the Garden of Eden or Prester John. Not a single Taíno has been baptized. No cathedral has been built. We know, too, that Fray Buil and Captain Margarit have mutinied and returned to Spain to tell all who will listen that Columbus is a fraud.

The danger to the admiral is real.

Caonabo sends messengers to other villages, including to my uncle, Behecchio, in the west, and to Higuayo in the east.

Hector tells us that Mayobanex, whose village is closest to *Isabela,* already has sent his people into hiding in the mountains, as has chief Guarionex.

"Warnings were also sent to Guacanagari, but we fear he won't heed them because he still thinks the admiral is his friend," Rodrigo says.

"This is terribly serious," Hector says in a near whisper. "To this day, I have nightmares about being paraded naked in front of hundreds of buyers at the slave market in Seville. I don't want that happening to your men and your women."

Anacaona pulls out her dagger.

"I need to sharpen this."

Chapter 41
A Terrible Idea

Messengers begin arriving at Caonabo's village saying mounted Spanish warriors are capturing hundreds of Taínos, mostly in the northwest part of the island.

Mayobanex and Guarionex send word that most of their people are safe, but many of Guacanagari's people have been captured, bound and taken to *Isabela* for shipment to the slave market in Seville.

"Columbus' most loyal friend is finding out the admiral's true colors," Anacaona says grimly. "Guacanagari is a stubborn old fool who has refused to fight the Spaniards, but even so, he and his people don't deserve this."

I feel sad for Guacanagari.

His only—and estranged—son died in battle, and is buried far from home without his father's prayers. Guacanagari trusted Columbus and believed the admiral would make him king of the island. He believed Christianity would save his soul and give him and his people eternal life. He abandoned our gods, accepted the Spanish God, and now he is being punished. Now, many of his people are bound for slavery—if they survive a terrible ocean crossing to Spain.

I say silent prayers to our gods to help Guacanagari and his people. I add a prayer to the Christian One God. I'm desperate.

As we help Caonabo's people—including my wife and baby son—flee to the mountains, I keep asking what can be done to stop this cruelty.

Even though Caonabo's people are likely to escape from this current slave raid, what will happen if Columbus sells 4,000 Taínos a year into slavery?

We pack our belongings and load them on the Andalusian horses, Count and Countess. Mencia won't ride the horses by herself so she will walk and carry our baby son. I wish I could travel with them, but Caonabo insists that I stay near him in hopes of finding ways to protect our people.

By now, only Rodrigo, Hector, Anacaona, Caonabo and I remain in the village. When I kissed Mencia and my baby son goodbye, I promised the gods I would do something to stop the Spanish slave trade. For me, the most important goal is keeping our people—and, most especially, my son—free.

"Is there nothing we can do?" I demand in despair as we gather once again around a fire outside Caonabo's hut.

"I could organize another army, and we can fight the Spanish—but in full-out battle we stand little to no chance," Caonabo says, discouragement in his voice.

We have no match for the Spaniards' weapons, even though we outnumber them many times over. We had hoped that hunger, sickness, mutinies, and failure to find gold would cause the Spaniards to simply pack up and sail away. But Columbus is a stubborn, desperate man determined to survive his critics' attacks.

Slavery is his solution.

We sit in a sad silence, hoping our gods—or someone—will help us find our solution.

"Only one person can stop this—Queen Isabela," Hector says. "She wants souls saved—not enslaved!"

Rodrigo shakes his head sadly, and says: "Columbus will claim that the only people they've captured are cannibals who can't ever be baptized because they've committed the mortal sin of eating human flesh."

"That's outrageous!" Anacaona says. "We mostly eat fruits and vegetables. We sometimes eat iguana, small rodents, birds and fish—but we never ever eat human flesh."

"Can no one challenge Coumbus' lies?" Caonabo asks.

I look at Rodrigo, and he looks at me strangely. His lips are pursed, his brow furrowed. He's slowly shaking his head.

What is he thinking?

"I have a terrible idea," he says in a near whisper. "I hate it, but it might be our only hope."

Before he says another word, I interrupt and say: "No. I won't go."

"You'll not go where?" Caonabo, Anacaona and Hector ask, all at the same time.

I don't answer, but Rodrigo says: "I'm suggesting that Guarocuya travel back to Spain. To court, to see his godmother. To tell her the truth. No one else can even get to see her, much less tell her the truth."

Hector looks at Rodrigo and says, "If this is your idea—sending Guarocuya back to Spain—you are right, it is a terrible idea!"

Rodrigo shrugs. "I know. I said so."

I silently agree with Hector. I remember that the queen wanted me to stay in Spain, living in luxury at her court, but I wanted desperately to come home. And now, with my marriage to Mencia and the birth of our son, I have even more reason to stay home. I want to flee to the mountains to be with them. Living in the mountains—even for years—wouldn't be a bad life.

"I can't think of any better ideas. Can anyone?" Rodrigo asks.

I don't want to go. I don't want to leave my wife and son and family and friends. I'm terrified at the prospect of another—hopefully two—oceans crossings.

"There's got to be another solution," I mutter.

No one answers.

My mind races: How long will we have a home if Columbus and his slavers aren't stopped? Will Mencia and my son and family be safe if slaving isn't stopped? Can anyone else stop slaving except the queen? Can anyone else reach the queen and tell her the truth?

I look into the eyes of Rodrigo, Hector, Anacaona and Caonabo.

"We all agree it's a terrible idea!" Caonabo says.

But it's the only idea we have. We sit in silence for many minutes, hoping and praying for inspiration. A better plan.

None comes.

"I'll go," I say in a whisper.

Everyone looks at me, but says nothing.

"I'll go," I say in a full voice.

"Your terrible idea is going to get Guarocuya killed, or sold into slavery," Hector argues.

Caonabo asks: "Why would Columbus allow Guarocuya to go to Spain? Why wouldn't he just sell Guarocuya into slavery? How can we be certain the queen will see Guarocuya?"

"Remember, Christians can't be sold into slavery," Rodrigo answers. "Columbus—and the entire royal court—saw Guarocuya baptized in

Barcelona, and they saw the queen become his godmother. King Ferdinand is his godfather. They gave him the Christian name Enriquillo in honor of Isabela's half-brother, the former king. It's unlikely that Columbus would dare harm the baptized godson of Isabela and Ferdinand."

His arguments are strong, but I wonder if we've made too many assumptions about Columbus being a good man. Why should we trust him again?

"Columbus has seen Guarocuya many times in the last year and never recognized him. How can Guarocuya prove he is the queen's godson?" Hector asks.

"The queen gave me a Bible written in Latin, and this ring," I say, showing the royal treasure I wear chained around my neck. "Columbus has only seen me as a painted native. I could wear one of the robes that Prince Juan or Princess Catherine gave me. I can ride into *Isabela* on one of our horses. I can say the Lord's Prayer in Spanish."

"I have one of the robes here," Anacaona says, almost in a whisper. "But I'm not agreeing to this plan—at least not yet."

"If Guarocuya is going, I'm going with him," Rodrigo says. "I can help him reach court."

"I am willing to go, too, but everyone—except the slaves—has to pay for passage back to Spain," Hector says. "How can we pay that? I have almost no money."

I chuckle and say, "The Count of Messina has given me 20 gold doubloons. I've never had use for gold before. Is 20 gold doubloons enough to pay for passage?"

"Five times over, probably" Hector says.

"So, it's agreed?" Rodrigo asks.

"It's agreed that this is a very terrible idea," Hector says.

"The only one who can agree to this terrible plan is Guarocuya," Caonabo says.

My mind races but finds no alternative.

"We have no better plan, do we?" I ask.

"The Spaniards will try to kill you," Hector says grimly. "They won't want anyone else going to court and telling the queen the truth. They'll just toss you overboard and laugh when the sharks eat you."

"That's why we're both going with him," Rodrigo says. "To guard Guarocuya—the Taínos only hope."

"That makes a terrible idea only slightly better—or even worse," Hector says. "I hope they don't try to sell me at the slave market again."

We watch the fire burn down in silence until Caonabo stands, hugs me, and says, "I fear you must do this—we have no choice."

"You're right. We have no choice. I will go."

"But you must return to raise your son, my grandson."

"I'm going to Spain to protect the Taínos, and most especially your grandson—my son."

Chapter 42
Descent into *Isabela*

18 February 1495

Anacaona returns Prince Juan's robe to me.

"I know you will put this to a good use," she murmurs.

We exchange knowing looks.

"I will try."

"I'm sorry we've come to this act of desperation. If you decide to change your mind—to not go—we all will understand."

"If I can reach the queen…" I say, my voice trailing off.

Tears well in the corner of her eyes. Now in mine, too.

"I need you to take care of my wife and child—and Caonabo," I tell her. "I don't know what we would do without his leadership—and yours."

"My foolish husband is going to travel at least part of the way with you to *Isabela,*" she says. "I'm not. We will have to part soon."

We have brought the horses back from the mountains, and will ride them to Mayobanex's village.

Hector and I ride on Count, while Rodrigo and Caonabo ride together on Countess. I have the robe and my other treasures packed in cotton cloth strapped to Countess.

We reach the last hill with a view of Caonabo's village, and we turn the horses so we can look back.

Anacaona waves at us, then turns and walks out of our sight. A wave of sadness hits us—something final about waving goodbye to her.

In less than three days, we reach Mayobanex's village, and are delighted to find him present, although the village is otherwise deserted. He's a brave man to stay so close to the center of the slave hunt.

"None of the Spaniards has left the village for a couple of days," he tells us in despair. "They've captured about 1,500 Taínos. All of them are tied to trees, or to each other. They're not given much food or water."

We tell Mayobanex of our plans to go to Spain.

He shakes his head in disbelief, but doesn't try to change our plans.

After scanning the scene, Rodrigo and Hector estimate that the slave ships will leave in two or three days. "We don't have much time," Rodrigo says.

We decide that Hector and Rodrigo will walk into the village. My entrance will be more dramatic—for a purpose.

As they leave, Rodrigo turns to me and says, "The more I think about this, the more I think this is a terrible plan—maybe worse than terrible."

"Not too late to back out," Hector tells me.

"Somebody have a better plan?" I ask. Everyone looks at the ground.

"Remember always that you are the queen's godson," Rodrigo says as he readies to leave for *Isabela.*

I shake my head and can't speak. I gesture that they should start their trip into *Isabela.*

"We will do everything we can to protect you," Hector says in parting, but I know there's little they can do if the Spaniards turn on me—and them. We will die together.

After we watch them reach the Spanish village, Caonabo and Mayobanex help me into the robe Prince Juan gave me many months ago. I wonder what he would think about what's happening in the colony he's to inherit. I take comfort in the fact that Mencia last wore the robe.

With their help, I mount Count, and the two chiefs hand me my treasures— the Bible, 20 gold coins, and the carved chess set. I touch the ring Queen Isabela gave me. I caress the dagger Mencia gave me. If found, I will claim it, too, was a gift from Prince Juan.

I repeat to myself silently, "You are Queen Isabela's godson. They won't dare hurt you. You are the queen's godson."

I pray to the gods. Our gods. Their God. I am terrified.

Caonabo looks up at me mounted on Count and tries to smile. Tears have welled in the great warrior's eyes.

Mounted on Count, I begin my descent into *Isabela.* I try desperately to control my trembling. I must act like a prince. The queen's godson. The king's godson.

Near the edge of the village, a young Spanish sentry steps from behind a tree and bars my path. He points a spear at me.

He is startled by my appearance—an Indian dressed in royal robes—mounted on a splendid Andalusian horse.

In clear Spanish, I tell him: "I am Prince Enriquillo, godson of Queen Isabela and King Ferdinand, and I demand to see my friend, Lord Admiral Christopher Columbus, viceroy and governor, and Admiral of the Ocean Sea."

The stunned sentry, not knowing what else to do, leads me into *Isabela*.

My appearance causes an immediate commotion throughout the village.

As a swelling crowd circles, me, I call out that I am the godson of the king and queen, and demand to see Admiral Columbus.

I spot Rodrigo and Hector standing at the edge of the crowd, and my trembling eases slightly. But I know they, too, are at risk should our plan unravel. They can do little to protect me should the Spanish try to capture me, but they would die trying.

In just moments, a stunned Columbus and his brother Bartholomew push their way through the crowd, and stand in front of me. They order the crowd to stand back, and a few Spaniards take a step or two back.

"Greetings, Lord Admiral," I say in a clear Spanish with just a slight quaver in my voice. "I am one of the six Taínos you took to Spain. You were present when four of us were baptized before the king and queen at court in Barcelona. I was given the Christian name Enriquillo, and Queen Isabela became my godmother, and King Ferdinand became my godfather."

"I…think…I…remember," the admiral says stumbling for words, his face showing puzzlement, and amazement. His brother's face shows a stunned fury.

I hear Rodrigo's voice call out: "I, too, was at court when this Indian and three others were baptized into the Christian faith."

"Preposterous! Prove this!" Bartholomew demands. "Prove this, or die!"

"Prince Juan gave me this royal robe," I say, holding my arms high for all to see the precious silk garment. "Princess Catherine also gave me a royal robe, and ask that I someday come to her court in London after she becomes Queen of England."

I show them the ring the queen gave me. Columbus looks at it closely, as does his brother. The admiral nods to his brother that the ring is real.

"Where have you been since we returned here?" Columbus asks.

I lie, and say: "I have been traveling all over the island. My godmother, Queen Isabela—your great benefactor—made me promise that I would return to her court one day and report to her on the progress of the salvation of the souls of my people—her subjects."

"Why have your come here today?" Bartholomew demands. "Why now?"

"I have heard that you have ships ready to return to Spain. That doesn't happen often. I wish to return to Spain now so I can honor the queen's command that I return to her court, and report to her. She is my godmother."

"When did you learn to ride a horse?" Bartholomew asks. "Most Indians are terrified of horses. Where did you get this horse?"

"A friend in Spain taught me to ride—and love horses. I rode a horse many miles across Spain with the Lord Admiral."

Columbus whispers to his brother that he remembers one Indian riding a horse when his troupe traveled from Palos to Barcelona.

For effect, I add that I rode horses with Prince Juan.

Bartholomew asks where I got a horse on the island.

"A Spaniard who returned to Spain left his horse here. I bought him."

"How did you buy the horse?" Columbus asks.

I show him my doubloons. The brothers, and all the Spaniards close enough to see, are astonished. A buzz passes through the crowd as the story of the gold spreads.

"How did you learn to speak Spanish?" Bartholomew asks angrily.

"The queen, as you know, has many scholars at her court. They helped me learn. I also attended mass every day with the queen, and the priests help me learn your language."

"You say you were baptized. Are you really a Christian?" Bartholomew demands.

I remember the Bible. I take it from my packet and hold it over my head for all to see.

"As I said—and the Lord Admiral was a witness—I was baptized at court. My godmother, Queen Isabela, gave me this rare, precious Bible, so I could continue my studies, and so I could help spread the gospel to my people, as she commanded me to do."

Columbus takes another step forward and says, "I remember you well now, Prince Enriquillo. Forgive me my forgetfulness, for you see I've been very ill. Our fleet will leave in two days. It will be very crowded, but if you wish to return to Spain to honor Queen Isabela's command we will be honored by your presence."

Bartholomew scowls, but says nothing.

I look again toward Rodrigo. His terrible idea just might work.

Or get the three of us killed.

My dagger remains hidden.

Chapter 43
The Slaves Gauntlet

I dismount and work my way through the crowd of curious Spaniards toward Rodrigo and Hector. Columbus, Bartholomew and Diego gather hurriedly to discuss my arrival and my wish to see the queen.

Rodrigo holds a finger to his lips, and whispers: "No matter what happens, don't interfere!"

"Why? What's going to happen?" I ask, alarmed by his words.

"Columbus and his men are going to decide which of the captured Taínos are going to be taken to the slave market in Seville," Hector says.

"Four ships are going, and there are about 1,500 captured Taínos here. Columbus wants to pack 125 Taínos per ship," Rodrigo adds.

"What? 125 Taínos per ship—plus a crew? That's impossible! Those caravels shouldn't carry more than 40 men!" I say.

"They're just going to pack them in the hold like livestock," Hector says.

"Two out of three of the Taínos captured are not going," Rodrigo adds, "the Spanish are going to line all of them up and pick the best ones—the men and women most likely to survive the trip and most likely to attract high prices at the slave market."

Hector adds, "I heard Columbus say he thinks young, beautiful, naked Indian women will attract the best prices."

I think of Mencia and thank the gods she is safe. I shake my head in disbelief and ask, "What will happen to the ones not going to Spain?"

"They will be offered to the Spaniards here as slaves," Hector answers. "Some beautiful women have already been given to the admiral's friends."

"Taínos not claimed will be set free," Rodrigo adds.

We watch in anguish as the captured Taínos are gathered in a makeshift corral surrounded by armed, mounted, jeering Spaniards. We hear cries of torment, pleas for mercy, and prayers to our gods.

Columbus and his men seem deaf to the pleas, the suffering, the prayers. Our gods do nothing.

Attempts at escape are met by sharp spears. We see some bodies lying in the corral, dead or comatose.

A man with a whip steps forward. It's Alonso de Hojeda.

A gauntlet of spear-carrying, jeering Spaniards forms, and Hojeda uses his whip to force the Taínos—one by one—to run through the gauntlet.

Columbus and his brother, Bartholomew, stand at the end of the gauntlet. At either side are two more makeshift corrals—one nearer to the sea for those selected for the slave market, and a second for those rejected.

Prodded by Hojeda's whip and the prodding spears, terrified Taínos pass through the gauntlet. Some can barely walk. Others are dragged, some begging, some unconscious.

At the end of the gauntlet, Bartholomew does most of the work, quickly directing each Taíno to the right or left. Slavery either way, but those going to Spain will face a horrid ocean crossing in the crowded, dark hold of a rocking ship—followed by life in a cruel, unknown, unforgiving land.

I can barely watch.

"Remember, do nothing!" Rodrigo commands. "You can't help here. Even the queen's godson can't stop this. But you can help at court if you can talk to Queen Isabela!"

Hector guides me to the edge of the village, away from the whip and the gauntlet. Revolted, I turn and vomit.

"It was a scene like this in Africa where I last saw my family," he whispers to me, tears in his eyes.

Even at a distance, we can hear the pitiful pleas, prayers, cries and moans of the captured Taínos, and the laughter and taunts of drunken Spaniards, Hojeda's whip cracks regularly.

After about an hour, Rodrigo joins us, and says, "Almost finished."

We force ourselves to return, to witness these acts of inhumanity. From one of the corrals, some 500 Taínos are being pushed toward the four caravels, destined to a slave market.

The second corral is surrounded by drunken, laughing Spaniards picking out slaves.

After about an hour, more than 300 Taínos are unclaimed, including eight women carrying their babies.

Hojeda opens a gate on the corral, cracks his whip, and says to a huddled mass of Taínos: "You are free to go! Run! Get out of here you wretched rejects!"

They climb over each other, fleeing up the bluff, never looking back, racing to the mountains.

To our shock, we see women drop their babies on the ground, and run.

"They're leaving their babies!" I cry.

"They are abandoning their newborns so they can run faster!" Hector says.

"Now, we can do something!" Rodrigo cries. "Now we must do something!"

He, Hector and I rush to the corral and gather up the wailing babies. I think of my newborn son, and pray to the gods for his safety.

Then I pray for the safety of our gods.

Spanish soldiers see us and bar our path, but Columbus youngest brother, Diego, rushes forward and orders the soldiers to let us pass.

"Someone has to do something about those babies!" he tells the soldiers.

In a few minutes, Diego and Dr. Chanca bring blankets we can wrap around the babies.

Chanca wheels his cart—his dead man cart—toward us, and we use it to carry the squalling babies to Mayobanex's village.

"We saw everything," Mayobanex whispers. "I had to almost tackle Caonabo and restrain him from running down there to try to stop the Spaniards."

"I am ashamed that I could do nothing!" Caonabo moans, his voice cracking. "I think it would be better to die than to witness that and do nothing."

"We all share the shame," Rodrigo says. "But there was nothing any of us could do! If you, Caonabo, had tried to stop them, the Spanish would only have had a greater victory to celebrate—the capture of the feared warrior Caonabo."

Even so, we all stare at the ground, mortified at what we'd seen and that we'd done nothing—that we'd been so powerless.

We have little time because the Taínos are being loaded into the caravels.

"We must go now," Rodrigo tells the chiefs.

Caonabo and Mayobanex promise us they will do everything they can to protect the babies, and to reunite them with their mothers.

As we leave, Caonabo stands and hugs me, tears flowing down his cheeks. "You must stop this! Your godmother must stop this!"

Rodrigo, Hector and I walk in stunned disbelief back to *Isabela,* knowing we will soon board one of the slave ships going to Spain.

"It's not too late to change your mind," Rodrigo tells me. "The voyage across the sea will be even worse than what we witnessed today. And your life will likely be in jeopardy."

"I'd never forgive myself if I didn't try to stop this madness." I remember that Columbus hopes to ship four thousand Taínos a year to the slave markets.

"We'll be by your side," Hector says. Rodrigo nods agreement.

I'm certain we will die together, but we'll die trying.

Chapter 44
Servants in Spanish Hell

24 February 1495

Rodrigo fears assassins, so he's gotten us berths on the ship Diego Colon commands. "He's as good to a friend as we'll find," Rodrigo says.

As Haiti disappears into the horizon, I look back at the home I struggled so hard to return to—and wonder if I'll see Mencia and my son again. And my parents, and Caonabo, Anacaona, Mayobanex, and the mountains and streams I love.

Rodrigo says Diego is traveling as Columbus representative to counter the tales the mutinous Fray Buil and Captain Margarit are spreading at court, and to help negotiate a treaty that will divide the so-called 'New World' between Spain and Portugal.

Rodrigo tells us the sovereigns requested that Columbus return to Spain to help with the treaty, but the admiral declined, and assigned Diego to perform the task.

Near the end of our first day at sea, Diego orders me to report to him at the bridge, and asks, "I recognized you. You lived with me for a while. Why didn't you tell me you're the queen's godson?"

"I didn't know who to trust." I can hardly tell him I was acting as Caonabo's spy.

"I can't blame you for that," he says. "Most people try to appear to be more than they are, and most would flout their ties to the queen."

I shrug.

He smiles. "You made quite the spectacle, you know, riding an Andalusian horse into *Isabela* wearing royal robes, waving the queen's Bible over your head, showing off gold doubloons and the queen's ring. And it worked—

nobody dared touch you! My brother, the admiral, worships the queen! Even Bartholomew didn't know what to do."

He shakes his head in disbelief and adds, "You're a brave man. Is there anything I can do to help you?"

I remember that Diego helped us rescue the abandoned babies, and earlier helped persuade his brother to free the three captive Taínos. I'm glad to know there is some humanity among the invaders.

I think for a moment, then answer: "Yes. Rodrigo, Hector and I would like to help take care of the Taínos."

"It's grim in the hold—dark, damp, dirty and crowded, and filled with excrement and vomit. It already smells dreadful. It's another level of Dante's Hell. Why would you volunteer to work in a chamber of Hell?"

"Rodrigo is trained in medicine. Hector has been a slave. I'm a Taíno. We want to help them. We want to do something good."

He looks around for possible eavesdroppers, and whispers, "I want you to know that I protested this slaving. But Christopher always listens to Bartholomew and never to me."

I am silent. My goal is to urge the queen to stop all slaving, but I don't want anyone but Rodrigo and Hector to know that.

"I'm afraid the slaves are going to die before we reach Spain. If you can help them survive, you have my blessing. You will need to work with Sergeant Cerberus. He's a soldier who's been assigned to make sure the slaves don't escape from the hold."

***

"You are certain you got that name, right?" asks an incredulous Rodrigo. "Sergeant Cerberus?"

"Yes. That's what Diego said," I answer. "Why are you amazed?"

Rodrigo and Hector exchange glances.

"Cerberus is a figure in Greek mythology—a multi-headed dog with a serpent's tail who guards the gates of Hell to prevent escapes," Rodrigo says.

"A terrible, despicable creature," Hector adds.

"Diego says we need to meet with him. He's in charge of keeping the slaves in the hold."

"Of course. He's guarding our gate of Hell," Hector says.

We seek out the sergeant, who is a burly, odorous, unclean man in his mid-twenties with a scraggly beard and one eye. A filthy, homemade eyepatch covers his empty eye socket.

"The captain assigned us to help the Taínos," Rodrigo tells him.

"You mean the monkeys?" the sergeant laughs.

"Yes," Rodrigo answers, barely hiding his anger.

"I know. The admiral's weak-kneed brother told me," Cerberus says. "Fine by me. Nobody else wants the job. I'm never going down there—the smell is already terrible. My only job is to make sure none of them escape!"

"If you'd let them out on the deck once in a while, I'd be willing to clean the hold so there's be less smell, and the Taínos would be healthier," Hector offers.

"No!" Cerberus barks. "My job is to guard the monkey slaves and make sure they never get out of the hold until we reach Spain."

"We'd like to bring the Taínos food and water, and to try to keep the hold clean," Rodrigo says. "I have some medical training, so I can try to keep them healthy. More would survive, and they'd fetch better prices."

"I guess we do want them to survive," the sergeant says, "especially the pretty young women."

"Why 'especially the pretty young women'?" Rodrigo asks suspiciously.

"I have a friend who runs a whorehouse," the sergeant says with a laugh. "I'm sure he'll pay good money for pretty females. Customers would line up! Maybe 20 customers a night per monkey!"

We look at him in shock, and—worse—realize he's likely right.

"I'm thinking about buying a couple young monkey slaves and starting my own whorehouse," he adds with a giant smirk. "I'll pleasure myself every night before I turn them over to the customers!"

Rodrigo blocks an angry Hector from striking Cerberus. "Be smart. We have a bigger mission," he whispers urgently to Hector in Taíno.

Hector backs away.

I try to calm the situation by asking the sergeant, "Is your name really Cerberus?"

He shrugs, smirks and says, "I'm a poor man from Extremadura. My family's name is Cerveli, but there's nothing special about that. I want to be special—that's why I traveled with the lying Admiral Columbus. But that didn't work out."

"What's that have to do with your name?" Rodrigo prods.

"I was at a whorehouse one time—one of my favorites—and this whore told me after we got done that my technique reminded her of a figure from Greek mythology. She said Cerberus was a very powerful and memorable figure, so I took the name. Makes me special! I wish I could read so I'd know more about him."

"It's a special name, alright," Rodrigo agrees.

"Don't you forget," Sergeant Cerberus says, "you're under my command. You're working for Cerberus. I'm never going down into that hellhole, but I'm in charge of it. And keep the hatch closed so the horrid smells don't escape!"

Antonio de Torres has overall command of the fleet, and he mistakenly tries to take a southerly route to Spain that leaves our sails mostly slack in calm seas for three weeks.

Temperatures remain mild, the seas calm. The Taínos suffer seasickness and depression, but none is seriously ill. Water and food are sufficient for all aboard—for now. We sneak extra supplies to the Taínos. Cerberus is drunk most of the time and leaves us alone.

That all changes when Torres finally points the fleet to the north, strikes gusty westerly winds, and we begin a torturous, late-winter trip across the North Atlantic.

Waves taller than our ships crash across the deck. Temperatures plunge. Fresh water becomes scarce. Food is rationed. Seawater seeps into the already damp hold, which is too crowded for anyone to work the bilge pumps. The Taínos have to lie non-stop in icy water. Their rations are the first to be cut.

The Taínos become so weak that they can't always pass the excrement bucket in and out of the hold. They moan, plead for mercy. Some pray for death—prayers that likely will be answered.

I climb often to the crow's nest to escape the smell, and even try to sleep there. But even at the highest point on the ship, in the strongest winds, the smell is there. I hold my shirt to my nose only to discover that the smell of vomit and excrement permeate my clothes. I smell my skin, and the odor is there, too. I wonder if I will carry it forever.

"Worse than anything Dante imagined," Rodrigo mutters.

But we never stop our work, although sometimes I have to vomit over the side of the ship after spending time near the hold.

Hector gives almost all his rations of water and food to the slaves. "I have no appetite." Rodrigo and I do likewise.

Diego gives us a dozen blankets—all his spares—which the freezing Taínos share.

The four slave ships travel together, and we begin to see bodies being thrown overboard from the other ships.

A school of sharks begins to follow the fleet.

Two days later, the first Taíno on our caravel dies.

"Combination of hypothermia, depression, dehydration, dysentery and seasickness," Rodrigo says of the dead.

'His prayers were answered,' I think.

Three more men die in the next week.

We have only a few moments for me to say prayers—Taíno death prayers—over each of the dead men before we drop their bodies into the sea.

Into the sharks' mouths. The school grows.

Three days later, Hector crawls through the crammed mass of humanity and carries the body of a young woman up to the deck.

She is the fifth aboard our ship to die.

Rodrigo finds part of an old sail, and wraps her naked body in it.

I think of my wife as I say Taíno death prayers over the woman's body. I pray especially to God of the waters, *Bagua Maorocoti,* and to *Maketaori Guayaba,* God of the dead.

Hector and Rodrigo look at me, I nod, and they lift the body and drop her into the ocean.

Sharks swarm.

Chapter 45
The Switch

Nearly every day there is at least one body that Hector must carry up from the hold to be buried at sea.

One morning, as I'm waiting by the open hatch for Hector to return with another body from the bowels of the ship, I hear my named called.

"Guarocuya, are you there?" a male voice calls out in Taíno.

I say nothing. I wonder if a god is seeking me.

"Guarocuya, are you there?" It's a human voice.

"Yes," I answer in a voice just above a whisper.

"Guarocuya, please help me."

"What, what do you want?"

"Please come to me."

"Who's calling me?"

"Guarocuya, I must talk to you. Please come here."

Hector passes me, carrying a body up the ladder, another young woman, a girl really.

Hector and Rodrigo often go deep into the ship's hold, but I try to stay near the hatch where fresh air from above can ease the stench. My main job is to carry the excrement/puke bucket up the stairs and dump it in the sea.

I look at Hector for guidance.

"It's alright," Hector says. "They'll make a path for you. They all know our names. No one down here will harm you. Especially you. I've told them you are going to see the queen to get all this stopped. They talk about you, and pray for you. They hear you say the death prayers. You are their ray of hope."

Ray of hope in this hell.

I reluctantly and slowly work my way through the prone Taínos, deeper into the stench, and the frigid ankle-deep water. Despite my efforts with the bucket, puke and excrement are everywhere.

Taínos reach out to touch me. Some quietly call out my name. I hear prayers.

May the gods bless you; I hear from all sides.

"Where are you?" I call out as I near the middle of the ship's bowels. My feet are soaked in four to five inches of icy water. Darkness blinds me.

"You are almost here, Guarocuya" he says. "Two people away."

I move forward. Wet, cold hands reach for my arms.

"Thank you for coming, Guarocuya! We all know what you've done for us—what you are trying to do for us. We hear you pray for the dead—you do that right above me. We pray along with you. And we pray for you."

I am overwhelmed and can barely ask, "What's your name?"

"I am Tuakiri. My wife is Hapori. Hector just carried her out. The gods took her, bless them!"

I can't talk.

"She died last night."

"I am sorry." Only a whisper.

"She is better off now. I will miss her forever, but death is better than this— and better than having her sold into slavery."

I remember Sergeant Cerberus' description of women slaves in Spanish whorehouses, and think Tuakiri is right.

"What do you want of me?" I ask.

"I want to know, Guarocuya, what you will do with her. What happens after Hector carries her away?"

"We'll cleanse her body and wrap her in cloth. Then I will say prayers to our gods, and then…then we drop her into the ocean."

I don't mention the sharks.

"That's what I thought. We hear you say death prayers above us after Hector carries a body out," Tuakiri says. "That's why I need your help."

"What do you want, Tuakiri?"

"I want to be there, Guarocuya! I want to say the death prayers for her— for my beautiful Hapori. She wouldn't be here except that she followed when the Spanish captured me. She could have gotten away—but she followed me!"

I'm dumbfounded.

"We can't do that," I whisper.

"Guarocuya, I must to say the death prayers for her! I beg you!"

In the grim darkness, I see tears flow from his eyes.

"You just can't do that!" I answer. I think of Cerberus, the foul dog-creature assigned to prevent escape from this Hell.

"There must be a way!" Tuakiri pleads.

"We can say prayers for her right here."

"I've already done that. I must say them over her before she goes into the sea. Wouldn't you do the same for your wife?"

I think of Mencia. He's right. Tuakiri should say his wife's death prayers.

I come up with a terrible idea—worse even than Rodrigo's terrible idea that we travel to court.

There is a way, I realize, but I don't want to think about it. It could jeopardize our mission.

What if Cerberus catches us?

My eyes have adjusted a bit in the gloom, and I see Tuakiri. He is about my age and height, though his body is but a skeleton.

His eyes beg for help.

"I must say the death prayers!" Tuakiri repeats.

I take a deep breath.

I realize I will never forgive myself if I don't help this man.

"This will dangerous for both of us," I whisper.

I pull off my hat, shirt and pants. After a moment's delay, I hand them to him.

"Put them on. Climb the stairs out the hatch. Turn to your left. Hector and Rodrigo will be halfway down the deck, cleaning the body and putting cloth around it. Hurry!"

As Tuakiri puts on my clothes, I tell him, "Both Rodrigo and Hector speak Taíno. Tell them what you—what we—are doing. They might become very angry—especially Rodrigo—but tell them that I want this to happen."

Without another word, Tuakiri climbs over me and other Taínos, and I hear him work his way toward the hatch.

Prayers on all sides.

I am naked except for my loin cloth and the queen's ring on the chain around my neck. There is no room for me to do anything but to lay down in the icy, filthy water. Someone passes me a wet, soiled blanket.

Everywhere in the darkness, Taínos pray.

They pray for Hapori. They pray for Tuakiri. They pray for me.

As I join the prayers, my mind fills with images of Mencia, Caonabo, Anacaona, my mother, my father, Rodrigo, Hector, and other friends.

I remember walking the trails through the mountains with my father and uncle. I remember fishing in the clear rivers. I remember the times before the Spanish came. I remember my mother's special hugs when all others thought I was dead. I remember my dead twin's sweet voice.

I think of my mother's strange embrace, and even think she is embracing me now, even though we are thousands of miles apart. She is trying to protect me, always.

I wonder if I will ever see Mencia and my son, Lokono, again.

Then I panic. What happens if something goes wrong?

Can I survive in this frigid hold? Could I end up at the slave auction in Seville? Have I condemned Rodrigo and Hector, too?

What if Tuakiri is caught? What if Cerberus discovers our ruse? What if Tuakiri decides to follow his wife overboard?

He said death was better than life as a slave in the hold—this Christian Hell. Will I take his place at the slave market? Could I survive long enough to reach the slave market? Have I placed Hector and Rodrigo in greater danger?

I cannot block fear from racing nonstop through my brain.

For now, lying in ice water, darkness and filth, I am a slave. I am not the queen's godson, not Mencia's husband, not my parents' child, not my baby son's father, not protected by my mother's embrace.

Just a slave. A monkey on his way to the market.

I hear Tuakiri, Rodrigo and Hector. They are almost directly above me.

"You're not Guarocuya! What do you think you're doing?" Rodrigo demands of Tuakiri in an urgent whisper. "Where is Guarocuya?"

"She's my wife," I hear Tuakiri answer meekly. "Guarocuya and I switched. He is letting me say the death prayers for her."

"Lower your voices!" Hector says, also in Taíno. "Cerberus is looking at us! He's coming this way!"

I hear heavy footsteps on the deck above me. I think I can even smell Cerberus.

I can hear every word they say.

"Don't say a word, whoever you are!" I hear Rodrigo say in Taíno.

"What's going on?" I hear the voice of Cerberus demand.

"Just tossing another body to the sharks," Hector says. "Be done in a minute or two. Guarocuya has to say prayers first."

"Let me take a better look," Cerberus demands. "Ah! She's a young one, and pretty, too!"

"What are you doing?" I hear Rodrigo demand. "Leave the cloth over her. Stop that!"

"Remember I'm in charge, and I'm just looking…maybe touching a bit," Cerberus says. "Lovely legs, eh? Young too! Sweet!"

"Stop that!" Hector calls.

"Now what are you doing?" Rodrigo demands.

"Just trying to get a better look. What a shame. I could have made a fortune with her!"

"She's dead, for God's sake! Stop touching her!" Hector demands.

"You fellows step back a bit," Cerberus says. "I need a bit of relief."

"What kind of monster are you?" Rodrigo shouts.

"Remember I'm in charge here!" Cerberus says. "Just give me a minute or two with her."

"Are you crazy—or just evil?" Rodrigo asks.

"OK, I don't even have to touch her. She's dead—she won't mind, will she?"

"Cover yourself back up!" Rodrigo demands.

"You're not going to do that, you monster!" Tuakiri screams in Taíno.

"Stop that you little monkey! Get off me! I don't care who your godmother is! I'm the boss here!" Cerberus yells.

"Rodrigo, pull him away. I'll deal with the sergeant!" Hector's commands.

"Hey—what are you doing?" Cerberus calls. "Leave me alone! Stop! Help! I can't swim…"

Silence for a just moment, then Rodrigo shouts: "Man overboard!"

I hear many running feet above me. Everyone in the hold is listening.

"What's going on?" Diego Colon's voice.

"Sergeant Cerberus was helping us," Rodrigo says. "A big wave rolled the ship, and he fell overboard."

"That's not what I saw," Diego responds in a quiet voice.

"Maybe he just slipped," Rodrigo shrugs. "Whatever, his last words were 'I can't swim'."

"Looks like the sharks made fast work of him," say a voice I don't recognize.

Diego orders: "Finish up with this girl's body. Quickly Then come see me. We need to talk."

I hear footsteps moving away, and then I hear Tuakiri say the death prayers for his wife. I listen, and hear her body splash in the water.

I'm shaking, but not just from the frigid water. What did I just hear?

After what seems like an eternity, I hear a commotion as the hatch opens.

"Thank you for all you do for us!" I hear Tuakiri say at the hatch door. "Even for what you had to do today—that man, that beast wanted to do a terrible thing!"

"We are sorry about your wife," I hear Hector answer. "Now hurry back to Guarocuya! Give him his clothes back! Say nothing about this to anyone!"

Tuakiri climbs over and around the other Taínos until he reaches me.

He takes off my clothes, and hands them to me.

He thanks me repeatedly, until I tell him to stop.

He hugs me. I feel warm tears on his cheeks. On mine too.

After quickly dressing, I scramble over and around the Taínos, reach the hatch and climb the stairs.

I dare not look back, dare not think about leaving all these people behind. I hear many thanks.

I shared their misery—if only for a few minutes—and now I can escape.

No longer a slave. But feeling guilty that I'm free again, and they're not.

A furious Rodrigo meets me at the hatch.

"What were you thinking—trading places with one of the slaves? You could have ruined our entire mission!"

"I just did what is the best thing I've ever done in my life!" I answer.

Hector and Rodrigo look at me in silence.

"What was Cerberus doing?"

"You don't want to know," Rodrigo answers.

"What happened to him?" I ask.

Hector looks at me and answers, "Like you, I just did what is the best thing I've ever done in my life."

Chapter 46
Trial

"You are under arrest!"

"Bind their hands behind them," the first mate tells three armed sailors.

They grab us, pull our arms and hands behind us roughly, and tie them together tightly with damp ropes. We don't resist.

We are roughly led to the bridge where we meet Diego Colon.

"You've been accused of murdering Sergeant Cerberus," he says. "There are witnesses who saw you push him overboard. In fact, I saw it happen from a distance."

"We can explain!" Rodrigo says.

"No, I'm sorry, you can't!" the first mate says.

"What do you mean we can't?" Rodrigo asks.

"You are a Jew are you not?" the first mate asks.

"Yes."

"Let me handle this, Lieutenant Sierra," Diego tells the first mate.

"We all know that Rodrigo is a Jew," Columbus' brother says. He points to Hector and asks, "You served one of the court rabbis, correct?"

Hector nods. "For many years, proudly."

"Did you practice Judaism?"

Hector nods, and says, "Of course."

"Were you ever baptized? Even after your rabbi converted to the one true faith?"

Hector shakes his head.

"So, you, too, are a Jew?"

"I promised to convert."

"So you are either a Jew or a false Christian—the kind our Inquisition punishes!" declares first mate Sierra.

Hector says nothing.

"By the Decree of Alhambra in 1492," Diego says, "all Jews were banished from Spain. So, neither of you is a resident of Spain, and you have no legal rights here on this ship, which is legally part of Spain."

Rodrigo and Hector are stunned, as am I.

"You are accused of murdering a Christian, and, under our law and the decree of my brother, the presumption is that he is innocent—and you are guilty," Diego adds.

"And the little Indian is a pagan," declares the first officer. "He, too, is presumed guilty!"

"Hang them! Hang the Killers of Christ! Hang the pagan!" All the sailors join the first mate's chant.

The first mate smiles at us, and shows three long ropes. He throws them over the yardarm.

Nooses.

"Hang them! Hang them!" the crew calls.

Diego holds up a hand for silence.

"Actually, the Indian is not a pagan," he says, and asks me, "it's true, is it not, that you were baptized?"

"Yes, it's true! I was baptized in front of the entire royal court at Barcelona. Queen Isabela is my godmother. King Ferdinand is my godfather. I am their subject. Rodrigo taught me to speak Spanish, and I've served as a translator between the Spanish and the Taínos."

"And you, as I recall, are of royal blood," Diego says.

"Yes. That's why Prince Juan and Princess Catalina gave me royal robes to wear. I am known at the Spanish Court as Prince Enriquillo."

The mood of the crowd eases.

Diego shows a slight smile, and says, "So, you have the legal right to testify and tell us what happened."

I realize the situation is complicated because I wasn't actually present. But I can't say that I switched places with a slave—I don't want to get him hanged, too.

Most importantly, I need to keep Rodrigo and Hector from being hanged.

"Tell us what happened, Prince Enriquillo," Diego says.

"A young woman, hardly more than a girl, died in the hold. Hector carried her out so we could say prayers over her, and then drop her in the sea—just like we've done with the other Taínos who've died. I read from my Bible."

"What kind of prayers—heathen or Christian?" the first mate asks.

I lie—because our survival is at stake. "Christian, of course"

"What prayer?" Diego asks, coaching. "The Lord's Prayer, perhaps?"

"Yes! That's right."

Diego nods, looking relieved.

But the first mate interrupts. "He's lying. Most of us on the ship can't read, and nobody has Bibles—only the priests. How can we accept that this Indian has a Latin Bible and can read from it? Preposterous!"

"Let me handle this, Mr. Sierra," Diego commands.

He turns to me and asks: "Were you using the Bible the queen, your godmother, gave you? The one you showed us at *Isabela?*"

"Yes. The queen gave it to me as a most precious gift so I could spread the gospel to my people."

Then I lie. "It was open as we read prayers over the girl."

"I just don't believe it!" the first mate says, interrupting. "Make him prove he can read from a Bible."

Diego looks at me and asks, "Can you get your Bible and read for us?"

I nod.

"Lieutenant, accompany Prince Enriquillo to his berth so he can retrieve his Bible, and show you he can read."

The first mate, unties me from Hector and Rodrigo, and pushes me back to my berth.

At my berth, I nod with my head toward my treasures, including the Bible.

Since my hands are still bound, Mr. Sierra picks up the Bible, and we return to the bridge.

Diego takes the Bible, finds Psalms, holds the Bible in front of me, and says, "Read this aloud. Loud enough for all to hear."

I look at the word and silently thank Hector for the reading lessons he gave me.

I read slowly:

Fader oure art in heve, i-halgeed be thi nome, i-cume thi kinereiche, y-worthe thi wylle also is in hevene so be an erthe, oure iche-days-bred 3if us

I look up, and see members of the crew crossing themselves. They are shocked to witness an 'Indian' reading a Bible written in Latin.

"What happened as you were reading this prayer?" Diego asks.

"In the middle, Sergeant Cerberus approached us."

"Had he been drinking?" Diego asks, helpfully. "We all know he was quite a drinker."

"He may have been, but I was so startled I can't be sure."

"Go on with your story."

"Cerberus reminded us that he was in command—that we must follow his orders. He pulled back the cloth that covered the girl. She was naked. He said, 'She's beautiful'. Then he started to touch her body—all over."

I look around and see looks of shock on the sailors' faces.

"Rodrigo told him to stop, but he wouldn't. He said he didn't take orders from Rodrigo. Cerberus then pulled the dead girl's legs apart. He said he wanted to see better."

"We're talking about a dead girl, right?" Diego asks.

I nod. I see faces full of revulsion.

"Then what?" Diego asks.

"Then he starts to pull down his trousers and says 'I'm going to pleasure myself before you dump her in the water. He said, 'She dead, she won't mind'!"

I hear a gasp from the men.

"I was stunned. I became furious and lunged at him!"

"I don't blame you! What he was doing was barbarous!" Diego says.

"God-forbidden!" I hear the first mate say.

Diego nods for me to continue.

"Cerberus screams at me, and threatens to throw me overboard—to the sharks! Rodrigo grabbed me and pulled me away, and Hector grabbed Cerberus."

All the crew are leaning toward me to hear better, and I speak louder for their benefit.

I continue: "We had pulled down part of the railing so we could more easily drop the girl into the sea, and Cerberus reached for where the railing normally is, and…and he fell into the sea. His last words were 'I can't swim'."

The men are silent.

"We yelled 'Man Overboard' but before anything could be done—the sharks had him."

No one says anything.

Finally, the first mate says, "Cerberus was a brute, he always was. We all knew that—a drunken brute who named himself because of how a whore described his love-making."

"And Sergeant Cerberus did all that during Christian prayers, while the queen's Bible was open," Diego says for emphasis.

Diego points to me, Rodrigo and Hector and says, "These men are not murderers—they are heroes!"

The stunned crew is silent.

Diego continues: "Rodrigo and Hector acted to save the life of Queen Isabela's godson, who is a devout Christian who carries the queen's Bible with him at all times."

I look and see sailors nodding agreement.

"Cerberus acted foully during Christian religious services," Diego adds. "He likely was drunk, acted barbarically during a Christian burial service, and caused his own—deserved—death."

"Untie these men," the first mate orders. "And take down those nooses!"

Chapter 47
Help, at Last

April 1495

Cadiz, Spain

After seven weeks at sea, Columbus' slave ships arrive in Cadiz—a sad spectacle.

Of the 500 slaves packed in the holds of the four caravels, fewer than 150 are alive. Rodrigo, Hector and I are despondent after having cast more than 50 bodies into the Atlantic Ocean. It's little consolation that the death count was worse on the other three ships.

The horror isn't complete: The surviving Taínos, most of them ill and many near death, are to be taken to Seville to be sold at the slave market.

Rodrigo learns that Bishop Fonseca, on the day of our arrival, sent a message to court, which is meeting in Madrid, asking for approval to put the Taínos up for auction.

"We must get to court and tell Queen Isabela what's happened!" I say.

But our departure is delayed by the plight of the survivors. Only Hector, Rodrigo and I speak Taíno, and we need to help the Taínos get off the caravels. They are a pitiful sight, made worse by the gawking of curiosity seekers. We carry many of the Taínos ashore. Some are diseased, some are starving, and some have lost the will to live. Even ashore, Tainos continue to die.

Rodrigo knows the prior at Cadiz's Franciscan monastery who agrees to care for the Taínos. But we spend precious days in Cadiz before we can begin our journey to Madrid and the queen's court.

We decide that Hector will stay with the Taínos and act as their translator. We give him six doubloons—half of our remaining gold coins. The rest we need to buy horses and supplies.

"Use the money to help the Taínos in any way you think best," Rodrigo says.

Hector hugs us goodbye, adding, "You are our last best hope!"

I'm depressed. We're not certain the queen will even see us—and we've already lost some 400 lives.

Rodrigo and I use four gold coins to buy supplies and four horses so we can ride, virtually non-stop, the nearly 400 miles to Madrid. Sleeping just four hours a night, we reach Madrid in eight days—a trip across Castile that normally would take weeks. We have two doubloons left, and Rodrigo reminds me that he has a fortune of his own, but no way to obtain the money until we find our friend, the Count of Messina.

We learn to our great disappointment that Fonseca's messengers arrived before us. Our delay at Cadiz was costly.

Late in the afternoon, tired, hungry and broke, we reach the traveling court headquartered at the royal hunting lodge of El Pardo at Madrid.

We search out the Count of Messina, our long-time friend.

A guard points us up a hill where the count is staying at a villa. As Madrid is small and poor, it isn't difficult to find the count's villa.

"Madrid was a Moorish fortress for hundreds of years until it was conquered by Alfonso VI in 1085. It's one of my least-favorite places for the royal court to meet," Rodrigo mutters to me.

We arrive exhausted, hungry and filthy, but we are greeted as conquering heroes—and members of the family—by the count and countess.

"We must see the queen as soon as possible!" Rodrigo says after quickly recounting the slave ships' ocean crossing and the pending auction of the surviving Taínos.

The count tells Rodrigo and me to rest while he arranges a meeting with Isabela and Ferdinand. The count says he has clothes Rodrigo can borrow, but nothing that would fit me.

"I will wear the royal robes that Prince Juan gave me. I have carried the robe with me for many miles," I say.

I happily shed the rancid Spanish sailors clothing. I remember that they are the same clothes I loaned to Tuakiri, the grieving slave.

The countess smiles and says, "With that robe, you will make a great impression at court. You can be presented at Prince Enriquillo, royalty from Hispaniola—and the godson of Ferdinand and Isabela!"

With a smile, she adds a command: "You must bathe, both of you, before your royal audience."

Between yawns, Rodrigo recounts to the countess all that had happened.

"Not only are we trying to save the poor souls going to auction in Seville, we need to stop slaving altogether!" he tells her. "Columbus hopes to sell four thousand Taínos each year."

After a wonderful hot bath and several hours of sleep, we awake to the count's news that Isabela will see us the next morning.

"The queen is delighted to hear of your return, Guarocuya, although she, of course, refers to you as Enriquillo," he says.

He adds that the king, as usual, is away from court hunting, so we will meet the queen in her chambers.

I'm pleased, knowing we have a better chance persuading the queen to our cause in an informal setting, rather than at a formal court session. King Ferdinand's absence may also help us. We doubt he will object to slaving.

Over a fine dinner, we recount for the count and countess our days since we parted, including the mutiny by Margarit and Buil, the battles between Caonabo and Columbus, and the slave roundup.

"Your gold coins were of great help," I finish. "We used six coins to pay for our passage on the slave ships. We gave six to Hector to help the surviving Taínos, we used most of the rest to buy horses and supplies so we could ride to court."

"I am so glad they were helpful," the count says. He adds that he felt a bit foolish giving me gold coins knowing I had no use for them in Hispaniola.

After the horrible weeks on the slave ship—and dropping bodies of innocents to the sharks—Rodrigo and I find comfort in the friendship and hospitality of the count and countess.

We feel a bit hopeful for the first time in many weeks. Hardly anyone in Spain is more powerful than the Count of Messina. Tomorrow we will have an audience with the queen.

For the first time in many nights, my dreams are not visited by Cerberus' ghost, nor the cries of the Taínos bound for slavery, nor the rancid smells of the slave ship, nor the site of sharks trailing us, awaiting their next meal. Instead, I dream of my wife and son, and sleep well.

I awake to guilt that I could so easily—if only for a night—forget the plight of my fellow Taínos.

Chapter 48
The Queen's Fury

The count and countess accompany us to a waiting room outside the Queen Isabela's chambers. I'm dressed in Prince Juan's robe, and Rodrigo wears fine silks borrowed from the count. Baths in Moorish pools help make us presentable.

As we wait outside the queen's chambers, Rodrigo asks the count what happened when Fray Buil and Captain Margarit returned to court.

"They created quite a stir," the count answers. "They went to King Ferdinand because they knew he would be more sympathetic to them than the queen. The king accepted everything they said as the truth. He never liked Columbus."

"What did they say?" Rodrigo asks.

"That Columbus had lied about almost everything—that there is little or no gold, no spices, and he hadn't reached India, or China or Japan. They said Hispaniola was just a remote island with no wealth. They said Columbus was brutalizing the Spanish colonists, even including those of royal blood."

"All that is true," Rodrigo says, "but Columbus was even more brutal to the natives—the Taínos. He even came up with a rule that in a dispute with the natives, the Christians would always be believed. He promised a bounty for anyone who captured Caonabo—the chief who burned *La Navidad*."

"Do you know this Caonabo? He's become famous in Spain," the countess asks.

I smile. "His daughter is my wife. I gave her the mirror you sent me."

"You married? How wonderful," the countess says, hugging me. "And she liked the mirror."

"She was amazed at it. Every time she looks at it, she's delighted."

"We have a son," I add, wiping a tear from my left eye. "He's about six months old now. I hope to return to him, and to Mencia."

"We will do everything we can to make that happen," the count says.

The count asks me why relations with the Taínos turned so bad? He reminds us that Columbus had been full of praise to the Taínos and their kindnesses.

"We were willing at first to be friends with Columbus, to give them food and shelter, and to learn about your One God," I answer. "All that changed, I add, when the Spaniards started stealing our women and food, and killing and maiming our men."

"I saw the ashes at *Navidad*," the count reminds us.

"Caonabo attacked *Navidad* after the Spaniards raped and pillaged," Rodrigo says.

I add that the Taínos had hoped that when Columbus returned on the second voyage he would make things better, but he didn't.

"The worst was the slave roundup," Rodrigo says.

Not wanting to think about the slave roundup, I ask how the officials at court reacted to Buil's and Margarit's stories.

"The king believed every word, and so did all of Columbus' many doubters," the count answers. "Fray Buil said Columbus should be given the title of Admiral of the Mosquitos. Columbus is now the subject of widespread ridicule. We feel sympathy for his sons—Diego and Fernando—who are pages in Prince Juan's court."

"Does Columbus have any friends left?" Rodrigo asks. I remember that Rodrigo was once one of the admiral's greatest admirers. No longer.

"The queen still supports him, although even she has her doubts," the countess says.

"Should we still be his friends?" the count asks.

Rodrigo says he once considered Columbus a friend and a visionary.

"But he's not found gold or spices, nor has he reached Asia—although he still claims he has. He's lost his moral compass. His treatment of the natives is worse than abhorrent—and the slaving has made me lose all respect for him."

The count and countess nod their understanding, and Rodrigo adds: "I no longer consider him my friend."

"I wonder how the queen will feel toward Columbus after you tell her about the slave ships?" the count asks.

The countess says Columbus will have nothing left if Isabela doesn't support him.

Our conversation is interrupted by a liveried servant who ushers us into Queen Isabela's personal chambers.

We bow low to Isabela, but she rushes to me and tells me to stand.

"My dear godson, I am so happy! I wondered if I would ever see you again! I pray often for you!"

The queen looks at Rodrigo. "I am also delighted to see you, my Jewish friend. Your work with and for my godson is appreciated!"

Isabela waves the four of us to sit with her at a beautifully carved wooden table.

"Tell me everything!" she commands. She is relaxed, her smile is beautiful, her mood good.

That is about to change.

"Your majesty, we don't have time at the moment to tell you everything—we will, of course, do so later, at your convenience," Rodrigo says. "We rode hard to tell you about the slave ships from Hispaniola, and to ask you to stop the auction in Seville of the few surviving Taínos."

The queen looks puzzled, and says, "I know about the ships. I received letters from both Admiral Columbus and Bishop Fonseca saying the Indians brought here on the ships are either man-eating cannibals or prisoners of war. In both cases, it is permissible for those captured to be sold as slaves. My husband and I granted permission for the slave auction to proceed."

"But they're not!" I declare, angered at the false claims.

"They are not what, dear godson?"

"Neither cannibals nor prisoners of war!"

"Those are just excuses Admiral Columbus is using so he can sell innocent people to make up for not finding gold," Rodrigo adds, a bit more calmly.

I vigorously nod agreement.

"The king and I signed an order just four days ago—on April 12—permitting Bishop Fonseca to sell the Indians at the market in Seville based on the premise that they were either cannibals or prisoners of war," Isabela says, alarmed. "Are you saying we were lied to?"

"Yes! They lied!" Rodrigo says fiercely.

"You should know that in all the time the Spanish have been on Hispaniola, not a single native has been baptized," the count adds.

"Please—please, act quickly to reverse that order, your majesty," I beg.

"Tell me more," she says in a commanding voice. She is no longer the loving godmother. She is the warrior queen who vanquished Islam from Iberia.

We tell her about Columbus' failures, and his plan to sell four thousand slaves or more each year to cover the lack of gold and spices. We tell her about the Spanish soldiers going into the interior of the island and capturing innocent men, women and children.

Her eyes flash with anger when we tell her about the Spaniards sorting—like cattle—which Taínos would be placed in chains and shipped to Spain, which would be given to colonists at *Isabela*, and which would be set free.

We describe the entire scene, ending with the mothers' terror and their abandonment of the babies.

"The women left their babies behind?" she asks in a whisper. "Those are my subjects! They are supposed to be under my protection!"

We tell her about the horrible conditions on the slave ships, with 500 Taínos crammed into the holds of the four small caravels.

We recount that the Taínos received little fresh water, and mostly they had only hardtack to eat, which they'd never eaten before.

"They were practically naked and with few, if any, blankets. They'd never known cold before, and then we sailed into the North Atlantic. Temperatures were freezing, and the waves higher than the ships. They all were sick, cold and despondent," Rodrigo says.

"Most died before we reached Spain," I add is a whisper. "And they are still dying in Cadiz."

"You're telling me that more than half of the Indians died on the trip?" she asks. "What did you do with their bodies?"

"We dropped them into the ocean," I say, tears in my eyes. "A school of sharks followed each of the ships across the ocean." I shudder.

The five of us sit in silence for a few moments, before the count says, "Your majesty, we need you to order an end to the plan to sell the few surviving Indians at the slave market in Seville."

She rises. In a calm, but chilling voice she says: "I told Admiral Columbus—in writing and in person—that his most important mission was to save the souls of the Indians. He has written me repeatedly how kind and gentle the Indians are, and how open they are to becoming Christians."

Rodrigo repeats that not a single native has been baptized in all the time the Spanish have been on my island.

We say nothing, afraid now of her gathering fury.

"The admiral has no gold, so now he tries to pay back his promises with men's souls," she says.

"Godmother, you must stop this," I plead again.

"You are right. I will immediately prepare new orders for Bishop Fonseca to stop this slave auction."

Chapter 49
Shadow of the Inquisition

Although Rodrigo and I are exhausted, we must ride immediately to Seville with the monarchs' order to halt the Taíno slave auction.

The count and countess announce that they will ride with us.

"I can help you obtain fresh horses and supplies along the way," the count says.

"You're not going anywhere near Seville and the Inquisition's castle without me!" the countess tells her husband. "It's much too dangerous!"

"Don't worry," the count tells Rodrigo and me. "The countess can outride most men in Spain!"

"You're going to have a hard time keeping up with me," she adds with a smile.

She's considered the most unconventional woman at court—perhaps in all of Spain—riding horses like a man, reading, writing, wearing light clothes while the other women at court dress in layers of heavy woolens, and talking to men like an equal—all to her husband's delight.

The count arranges for us to have eight horses and plentiful supplies. We plan to sleep no more than three hours a day.

Time is our enemy. No matter how hard I try not to, my mind fills with images of my fellow Taínos being paraded naked at the auction and sold to Spaniards for all kinds of purposes.

The monarchs' order permitting the Taíno slave auction was signed five days earlier, and the queen says that order was sent the same day to Seville by royal messengers.

Our hope is that the royal messenger didn't ride as urgently as we will. Even so, a five-day head start will be difficult to overcome.

At our first camp site, Rodrigo whispers to me: "The count is taking a grave risk. He has avoided Seville for many years."

My mind flashes back to the count's story. His father and other leaders in Seville try to oppose the Inquisition when it started. Eight of them were arrested, tried, convicted and burned at the stake—among the first of thousands taken to the stake in Seville. Each of the eight men's sons also were condemned to burn at the stake. The count, aided by his long-time friend King Ferdinand, has been hiding under an assumed identity most of his life.

Inquisitors in Seville hunt him still.

I look over at him as he builds a fire. I'm afraid to even thank him for his help. Both he and the countess understand the grave importance of stopping the slave auction—but they are both putting their lives at risk at the very heart of the Spanish Inquisition. I silently pray to both my Taíno gods and the Christian One God to protect them.

Their presence is invaluable. With the count and countess at our side, all city gates open easily as we travel through Toledo, Ciudad Real, Cordoba and smaller villages. Fresh horses are given to us with no questions asked. Food and shelter are offered at all points—benefits of riding with the great Count and Countess of Messina, friends of the king and queen.

After seven and one-half days of hard riding and little sleep, we reach Seville and ride directly to the slave auction in the Plaza de San Francisco. We ride through the shadow of the great Seville cathedral, whose builders said, "Let us build a church so beautiful and so grand that those who see it finished will take us for mad." Almost everything about Spain seems mad to me.

The count, the first to reach the auction, dismounts and rushes to the platform where slaves are auctioned. We quickly follow him up the wooden steps.

No one is here.

No slaves. No masters. No auctioneers. No gawkers.

Most importantly, no one to receive and act on the queen's order.

The countess spots a young soldier standing in the street watching us, and she races down the steps toward him. We follow.

"Have the Indians been sold?" she demands of the soldier.

"It's all over," he answers. "You're too late to buy one."

We stare at him.

"All of them were sold yesterday. A big crowd gathered to see the naked Indians."

"All of them were sold?" the countess demands.

"Weren't that many," the soldier answers. "You didn't miss much. Most of them looked sick, and too small to do much work. That's all I know."

As we walk away from the soldier, the count suggests we go to Bishop Fonseca's office, but the countess tells her husband: "No. Fonseca is too friendly with the Inquisition. He's made a fortune turning people into to the Inquisition. He may even know that they're looking for you."

For a moment, we stand silent and disillusioned, not knowing where to turn before Rodrigo suggests, "Let's find Hector!"

"Where would we be?" the count asks.

"I told him we have friends at the Monastery of Santa Maria of the Caves in Triana, and he likely could stay there," Rodrigo answers.

The count's face blanches.

There's only one bridge across the river, and it's guarded by the Castle St. George, the Inquisition's headquarters.

"Too dangerous!" the countess declares.

But the count mounts his horse, grabs the reins and says, "We must chance it."

He rides off toward the bridge before we can stop him.

We quickly reach the Seville side of the Guadalquivir River, and the great cobblestone-covered wooden bridge that crosses into Triana.

The Castle St. George towers on the river's bank on the opposite shore.

"We're not even sure that Hector is over there!" Rodrigo says when he and his horse catch up with the count.

"We have to chance it!" the count says, spurring his horse onto the bridge.

The count's bravery is contagious, and we follow him.

"Ride with the flow," he tells us, "so we don't attract attention."

I'd like to spur my horse to a full gallop, but I know the count is right. We need to blend in with everyone on the crowded bridge.

We guide our horses on the far side of the bridge, hoping the guards at the gate and atop the castle don't notice us.

I'm shaking with fear. I glance at Rodrigo—he has to be wondering if his father is yet a captive in the castle's dungeons, of if he has died on the Inquisition's rack after his body was pulled apart, inch by inch.

Our horses' pace matches those walking across the bridge. We are slowed by farmers pushing small carts of goods into the city. But we do not complain or call out. We just thread our way slowly across the bridge, through the shadow of the Inquisition's castle.

The slow pace does not match the racing of our hearts.

"Don't look up," the countess whispers.

But we know we are being watched. The Holy Office of the Inquisition watches everyone.

I can't help but think: the count has already been condemned to death. Would they condemn us, as well, just for being with him?

Finally, we reach the western side of the bridge. We are in Triana.

We glace behind us. No one is chasing us.

Not yet, anyway.

We turn a corner—finally out of sight of the castle—and spur our horses up the *Callejon de la Inquisition.* Ahead, we see the narrow cobblestone street leading to the Monastery of the Caves.

We tie our horses to a wooden fence, rush inside, ask a startled monk if he knows the whereabouts of Hector—"a giant black man." The monk points to a small cell at the top of a staircase.

We race up the steps, and find Hector sleeping on a mat on the floor in the tiny, bare cell.

Rodrigo shakes Hector awake.

"You finally made it," Hector says, rubbing sleep from his eyes.

"We got an order signed by the queen and king to stop the auction," Rodrigo says.

Hector throws both of his big hands in the air and says, "You're a day late."

"We know," the count says sadly. "We went straight to the auction. What happened to the Taínos?"

In a voice deep with despair, Hector answers, "Many died before we even left Cadiz. The rest were sold yesterday."

"Died?" I whisper.

Hector reminds us that many Taínos were barely alive when the slave ships docked in Cadiz.

"Many preferred death to living as slaves in Spain," Hector says. "They stopped eating and drinking."

I'm not surprised. I, too, would rather die than be a slave in a foreign land. I didn't want to live as a guest in Queen Isabela's court—much less as a slave.

Hector tells us that about 60 men and 20 women finally reached the slave auction.

Of the more than 500 humans crammed in the holds of the four tiny caravels, just 80 survived to reach the auction.

"Who bought the Taínos?" the countess asks.

"Admiral Juan Lezccano Arriaran bought fifty of the men—the only healthy-looking Taínos—to work in the royal galleys," Hector answers. "The rest of the men were taken one at a time by men all across Andalusia."

"What about the women?" the countess asks, her voice barely audible.

"They were bought by disgusting-looking men," Hector answers.

I remember Cerberus' prediction that the women would be bought by whoremasters.

"I only had one gold coin left," Hector adds. "That was just enough to buy one of the small males."

"You saved one?" I shout.

Hector smiles, and gestures for us to follow him to the next cell.

"Tuakiri!" I yell as I come face-to-face with the young Taíno.

I tell the count and countess that Tuakiri is the Taíno I switched places with so he could say death prayers for his wife.

"That stunt almost got the three of us hanged!" Hector says, pointing a finger at me. "I'm proud of you!"

Chapter 50
Glory's End

After a few days' rest, the six of us begin a return trip to the royal court at Madrid. We want the queen's help in tracking down and freeing the Taínos sold at the auction – and stopping further slave ships.

The prior of the monastery loans the count monk's robes, and wearing the disguise he safely the crosses the bridge guarded by the Inquisition's castle.

The five of us closely follow the count across the bridge. We are mounted on horses with Tuakiri clinging fearfully to Rodrigo on a gentle gray horse. Once safely across the Guadalquivir and inside the city walls, the count sheds his robe and mounts his horse, which the countess had led across the river.

We race out of the city, hoping to never again see the towering castle of the Inquisition where so many had been condemned. Hoping never again to see Seville's slave auction.

The queen sees us the morning after we return to Madrid.

We introduce Tuakiri to the queen.

"He is the only one we could save," the countess tells the queen.

Rodrigo adds that Tuakiri's young wife died aboard a slave ship. We don't tell the queen about Cerberus' horrific antics over the dead woman's body. Rodrigo does tell her that changed places with Tuakiri so he could pray over his wife's body before it was dropped in the sea.

Isabela rises from the chair and bows to Tuakiri.

"I am so sorry for what we've done to you and your people—and your wife," Isabela says, tears in her eyes. "I am horrified by all that has happened."

She turns to me and bows, saying: "I am proud of you, my godson."

Later in the day, Queen Isabela signs orders that Admiral Arriaran is to free the 50 Taínos he bought to work in the royal galleys—but war is on and the ships are scattered. She issues another order that all the other slaves sold at the auction are to be found, freed and returned to Hispaniola.

When King Ferdinand returns from a hunt, we recount all that had happened.

"They didn't attract good prices at the auction?" Ferdinand responds. "I'm not surprised. None of Columbus' schemes work. He promises gold, but delivers mosquitos. You know, his nickname is now 'Admiral of the Mosquitos'."

Queen Isabela, once Columbus' most important supporter, looks bleakly at her husband, and says, "Columbus was supposed to save souls, not sell slaves."

"Columbus is a complete failure," the king responds. "He can't even operate an efficient slaving operation! Only 80 survivors out of 500. Everyone knows you need to have at least a 50 percent survival rate to make money!"

"Stop such talk, dear husband!" the queen says. "I worry about saving souls while you think only about profits!"

"Your heart is too good, dear wife, but all your support for your friend Admiral Columbus has only caused us grief and lost us treasure," the king retorts. "Now we have this failed slave operation."

"Perhaps you should order Columbus home, and give someone else command of the colony on Hispaniola," the count suggests.

"I would love to do just that, my friend," the king says. "But—unfortunately—we are in treaty negotiations with the Portuguese over a boundary line between our territory and theirs. If the Portuguese find that Columbus' claims are nonsense, we'd lose our bargaining position. While we're negotiating, we must continue to claim that Columbus has found a route to India, if not India itself."

The count sighs and nods agreement.

The king continues: "Not only do we have to deal with the Portuguese, the pope—our treacherous friend Rodrigo Borgia—actually named Columbus in the papal bull that gives Castile the right to claim all lands we discover that aren't the property of another Christian prince. If Borgia learns that Columbus is a fraud, we could lose those rights. We know we can't trust Borgia—so we're stuck with Admiral Columbus—for the time being!"

"But we are going to punish him," the queen adds quietly.

"How, your majesty?" the countess asks.

"We have decided to end Admiral Columbus' monopoly on commanding trips to the New World," she answers.

King Ferdinand nods, and adds, "We have just signed formal orders. Columbus is no longer in command of all transactions in the New World. From now on, the queen and I—with help from Bishop Fonseca—will approve all trips to the New World—not Admiral Columbus."

After we return to the count's villa, Rodrigo asks what the monarchs' order means for Columbus.

"It means," the count answers, "Columbus' days of glory are over."

Epilogue

February 1447

Santo Domingo, Hispaniola

A young guard brings me a bucket of water, rags and soap.

"Wash up," he orders. "The viceroy doesn't want you smelling up his office."

I don't argue or ask questions. I haven't been able to wash myself in weeks. Even as the guard watches, I rip off my loin cloth, plunge the rags into the bucket, wet myself all over, and scrub my body with the precious soap. What pleasure!

"Don't you want to know why the viceroy wants to see you?" the guard asks me.

I shrug.

Whatever the reason, I get a bath. Whatever the reason, I have no choice. I've learned to ask no questions, expect no mercy.

"He's been reading what you've been writing," the guard continues. "He's really angry!"

What's he going to do? Throw me in prison? Burn me at the stake—finally?

The guard leaves momentarily before returning with an old cotton shirt.

"Put this on," he commands. "The viceroy hates seeing naked Indians."

Two more guards arrive, each carrying chains. Irons for my legs and arms. I don't resist as they lock them on me.

The three guide me outside into the square. The viceroy's office is on the far side.

I haven't felt sunlight in—I can't remember when. The light nearly blinds me, but I love it!

"What are you smiling about?" one guard snarls. "The viceroy is none too happy with you! You may have a flogging coming!"

I can smell the sea! I can see the sky! There's the Ozama River. I remember that Columbus built on the eastern side, but the new viceroy has moved his headquarters to the western side of the river. The walk across the square is wonderful, even in irons.

Without fanfare, I'm pushed into Viceroy Lopez de Cerrato's office.

While most buildings here are squalid, the viceroy's office is regal—fresh flowers, large paintings, beautiful windows with glass. The viceroy is, after all, the representative of Emperor Charles, the grandson who inherited the vast Spanish Empire from Isabela and Ferdinand.

Giant portraits of Emperor Charles and Empress Isabela hang behind the viceroy's ornate, carved wooden desk.

The viceroy doesn't rise, doesn't look at me. I see my manuscript on his desk.

A guard prods me in the back and whispers: "Bow, stupid!"

I do. I am at this man's mercy.

"Your excellency," I say in Spanish.

He raises his eyes and looks at me, loathing in his black eyes.

"It's illegal for Indians to learn to read or write," he begins. "Yet you have written a detailed history of our first viceroy. Explain yourself!"

I'm surprised. The fat priest had told me that Emperor Charles had requested that I write the story. The viceroy had to know.

"Most of my men can't read or write, but I'm expected to believe that you—you scrawny old Indian—can write this story."

Ah. The problem isn't that I wrote my story—it's that it's too well written. Too accurate. No 'Indian' can be so intelligent. I surprised the viceroy.

"Explain yourself!" he repeats.

"Your excellency, I was writing at the emperor's request."

The truth in my answer only infuriates him further.

"Spaniards should write our own histories. Victors write history, not the losers. You lost!"

I'm afraid to respond.

"What you've written no one should see," he says. "I'm thinking of burning it."

"But the emperor…" I begin, but the viceroy holds both hands up to silence me.

"I know! Columbus' heirs are suing, claiming the Admiral was promised a percentage of everything he discovered while exploring for Isabela and Ferdinand. Emperor Charles wants this—your foul account—as evidence that Columbus was a fool, liar and a charlatan. But what you've written is heresy, it is treasonous! Dangerous if it falls in the wrong hands."

It's the truth! I want to shout. But I don't. I don't want to be flogged again. The scars still burn.

The viceroy paces around his office. He stares at me. He stares at the portrait of the emperor.

"I am going to send this—this heresy!—to the emperor with the suggestion that only he read it, and that he burn it after he does so," he mutters, more to himself than to me.

He points to the guards, and says, "Return this heretic Indian to his cell and make sure he's got nothing to write with! I'll let the emperor deal with him!"

Many months later, the viceroy is angered and frustrated to learn that Emperor Charles has read my account and wants me to keep writing. Charles wants more details of the events that led up to Columbus being arrested, placed in chains, and shipped back to Spain for trial.

"I have to keep you alive so you can continue to lie," the viceroy says, anger and disappointment in his voice.

Through my prison window I stare at the sky at night. Each star is one of our dead. I hope soon to join the campfires.

Afterword

In June 1538, Pope Paul III attempted to settle the long-simmering debate over whether Indians had souls.

He issued the bull *Sublimis Deus* declaring that "Indians were human beings." The pope further ordered that the natives "were not to be robbed of their possessions," and he ordered automatic excommunications for anyone who failed to abide by the new ruling.

Matters worsened when the Spanish court successfully pressured the pope to annual his bull.

After Paul annulled his bull, the bull *Inter caetera*, issued by Pope Alexander VI (Rodrigo Borgia) in 1493, continued to allow Spain to claim ownership of any lands not already controlled by a Christian prince. With that papal license, Spain created an empire on "which the sun never sets"—an empire that doomed many indigenous people.

The pope's ruling came too late for the people who had made first contact with Europeans on Hispaniola. By 1538, they were all but extinct.

Yale University studies estimate that the native population of Hispaniola when Columbus first arrived was somewhere between several hundred thousand to over one million humans. By 1514, only some 32,000 survived, according to William Keegan's "Destruction of the Taino."

The Spanish cleric and writer Bartolome de Las Casas—in his *A Short Account of the Destruction of the Indies* (published in 1552)—claimed there were but 200 natives on Hispaniola in 1542. And "within a decade or two of that, they were extinct," wrote historian Kirkpatrick Sale.

The natives died from disease, enslavement, starvation, murder and suicide. Their DNA exists today only in parts of Hispaniola's mestizo population – the mixed blood from the heirs of the Conquistadors and black slaves imported from Africa.

In 1505 (the year after his wife, Queen Isabella, died) King Ferdinand sent the first slaves to the New World – one hundred "negro" slaves from Spain to Hispaniola. In 1518, Emperor Charles (grandson of Ferdinand and Isabella) abolished the provision that only slaves born under Christian dominion could be sent to Spanish colonies, thus opening up the direct import of slaves from Africa to the Spanish colonies.

Maybe most importantly, Pope Borgia's bull *Inter caetera* lives on today.

In 2022, Pope Francis made what he called a "penitential pilgrimage" trip to Canada to apologize for the "evil" of the Catholic Church's role in a residential school system in which generations of indigenous children were forcibly removed from their home and forced to attend church-run, government-funded boarding schools to assimilate them into Christian, Canadian society.

Some say he didn't go far enough. Indigenous peoples have often demanded that the pope take responsibility not just for abuses committed by individual Catholic priests and religious orders, but for the Catholic Church's institutional 15th Century religious justification for European colonial expansion to spread Christianity.